INSTALOVE FALL FESTIVAL

COLLECTION

KATE TILNEY

Hunter

LOVE AT THE FALL FESTIVAL

KATE TILNEY

ONE

OLIVE

Driving my car over the crest of the hill, I gasp.

"What? What's wrong?" Laurel, my best friend, asks over the car's Bluetooth speaker. "Did a deer jump out of nowhere? Did you blow a tire? Did you suddenly realize you've made a terrible mistake?"

I roll my eyes even though she can't see me from her office in New York City. "Why does a gasp have to be something bad?"

"In my experience, it usually is."

"That's a pretty cynical way of looking at life."

"Just like packing up and heading to Vermont for the Fall instead of taking a good job at a Fortune 500 company is a crazy way of living your life."

"It's not crazy," I reply defiantly. "And I'm not crazy either."

Though, in Laurel's defense, both of my parents do think I'm nuts. I earned my MBA last spring. After, I spent the summer interning at a prestigious investment firm. Everything was going well. As my internship came to an end in early August, I was positive I'd be offered a permanent position.

Then, one night while fighting yet another bout of insomnia in the city that doesn't sleep, I found myself doing what most twenty-four-year-olds do when they can't sleep. I clicked on random links on my cell phone.

I was reading through a list of the top ten places to get an apple cider doughnut when I stumbled upon Ferguson Family Orchard. Nestled in the foothills of the Green Mountains, the orchard has been owned and operated by the same family for more than one hundred years. As I read about how many apple cider doughnuts they sell a year, I happened to notice the words "NOW HIRING" on the top of their page.

I clicked. Saw a job listing that seemed to be written just for me. And now, here I am, driving into paradise. Thus the reason for my gasp. Even though the leaves are just starting to turn red and orange, this is maybe the prettiest place I've ever seen. The photos were incredible, but they didn't do it justice.

"So"—Laurel interrupts my thoughts of rapture—"tell me again what exactly you'll be doing there."

I sigh. We've been over this a dozen times. But I suppose once more won't hurt.

"The orchard has asked me to take a one-season contract to help them drum up more business." My heart flutters as I think about all the opportunities ahead of me based on the emails and phone calls I've exchanged with the matriarch and patriarch of Ferguson Family Orchard.

"They have great local attendance, but they want to tap into the regional market more."

"Entice yuppies from New York City."

"And then some." My face bursts into a grin. "I also think they might have some potential for national markets with their products."

"So you won't be picking up bruised apples and holding ladders for visitors?"

"Well, I'm sure I'll be doing plenty of that too."

"Is that really your job?"

I answer her question with another. "Isn't that what it means to be immersive in a market? During my internship, I spent time on the stock market floor even though I was in the marketing department for an investment firm."

"The stock market floor isn't exactly the same as an apple orchard."

"Finally we agree on something!" Even if our meanings are different, at least we can both agree that working in a stuffy building with a bunch of stressed out people is completely different from working in the outdoors. "I'll be banking on happiness instead of speculation."

Laurel lowers her voice. "Is this about your grandfather?"

My heart pangs at the mention of him. "This is about finding what I'm supposed to do with my life. Besides, it's only a few months. If it doesn't work out, I can always come back to New York."

And I'll just be another cog in the machine. I dismiss the possibility from my mind. It's too depressing for such a pretty place.

It's then I see a sign for Ferguson Family Orchard.

Barely. It's pretty small and faded. Well, that's one easy fix we can make. When I reach an oversized farmhouse, I pull to a stop.

"Oh, Laurel. This place is stunning. Let me snap a photo for you."

Hopping out of the car carefully so as not to scuff my new ankle boots, I step backward. I want to get the house and some of the trees and mountains in the background. Once she sees this place, Laurel will have to concede that I didn't leave the city for nothing.

"Just give me one more minute." I take another step back. "I just need to—oof—"

I collide with a hard wall that reaches out to hold me upright. Spinning on my overpriced boots, I come face to face with a man. Not a wall. I forget to breathe as I raise my gaze up his body. Hard muscles are covered in a flannel shirt. The top button of his shirt is open, revealing a sprinkling of dark hair. His square jaw is covered by a well-groomed dark beard.

As my eyes lift to his, my heart pounds in my ears. This man has the most intense dark brown eyes I've ever seen. No, they're not just intense. They're furious.

Somehow, that snaps through the haze of my libido.

"Laurel, I'll have to call you back." I hang up the phone and tuck it into the back pocket of my skin-tight jeans. "Sorry. I wasn't looking where I was going."

"Obviously." Even with a frown, this man still has one of the most handsome faces I've ever seen. "Haven't you heard that it's dangerous to operate a motor vehicle—or walk—while talking on a cell phone?"

"I was using Bluetooth."

He arches a dark brow. "It's not about hands-free devices. It's about the distraction of the conversation."

"Well, I'm off the phone now." And why are my palms sweating like I've been called to the principal's office? I guess, in a way, it does feel like I've been called to the principal's office. Wiping my hand on my jeans, I thrust it out. "I'm Olive Murray. I'm the new manager of business development."

He doesn't take my hand but instead gives me a slow, appraising look. I can practically feel the heat from his eyes as it covers each inch of my body. And, darn it all, the butterflies in my stomach are flapping a mile a minute. How can I possibly be attracted to a guy who is staring at me like I'm the scum of the earth?

"I know your type." He meets my gaze again. "You've been online you saw a bunch of 'killer' photos. Ones you just had to recreate for yourself."

"That's not why I'm here."

"I hope not. Because this has been my family's business for generations. And I intend to keep it my family's business for generations to come."

Recognition flashes in my brain. "You're Hunter Ferguson."

"I am."

The oldest of two children, and the only son. He just retired from the military—I can't remember which branch. And, he doesn't want me here.

Hunter takes a step back. "I'll let my parents know that you made it."

And he disappears into the house. I let out a breath

and press a palm to my chest. My heart is still racing under my fingertips.

Oh, this could be trouble. Big trouble. Not only does Hunter Ferguson already hate me, but I might have a crush on him. Maybe Laurel is right. Maybe I have lost my mind.

TWO

HUNTER

After literally running into the big city woman my parents have hired—without discussing it with me first—I corner them in the kitchen of the main house.

"Your savior has arrived."

"Don't be crass." My mom grabs my chin and forces me to look at her like I'm three instead of thirty-three. "I know you might not agree with this decision, but I expect you to be polite."

"Too late for that," I grumble under my breath. "I ran into her while she was nearly breaking her neck."

I shake my head thinking about the pointy high-heeled boots she was wearing. I bet those things cost more than my truck. Granted, I'm man enough to admit I liked what those heels did for her legs. And her body. I got a good enough feel of those hips when I was holding her upright to know she has a body that could drive a man insane.

Which is unfortunate. It'll be pretty damn inconvenient if I can't get that shapely body of hers off my brain.

"What do you mean she was breaking her neck?" Dad asks from his stool at the island.

"She was doing a photoshoot with her cell phone while wearing a pair of heels not suited for country life."

"Well, I hope you helped her take her photo," Mom says. "That would be the gentlemanly thing to do."

"Who said anything about being a gentleman? I am a soldier."

"You're a retired soldier," she corrects. "And I raised you to be a gentleman."

Shaking off the comment, I reach into the fridge for the jug of filtered water.

"I don't get why you suddenly want more regional visitors." I slam the refrigerator door harder than necessary after refilling my water bottle. "You showed me the ledgers. We're operating in the black. We even have money to make some improvements without taking out a loan at the bank. What gives?"

"Your mother and I have been talking about this for a while." Dad pours himself another cup of coffee. I happen to know it's decaf because my mom subbed it out while he wasn't looking. But if he doesn't know, and doesn't care, there doesn't seem to be any point in enlightening him. "We want to leave a lasting legacy for you and your sister."

"Sienna and I can do just fine on our own."

"Sienna is still away at school," Mom reminds me. "And you've only been home for a couple of months."

Like I need a reminder of that. "I still think you

could've given us the benefit of the doubt. We've spent our life here. We don't need a stranger's opinion."

"Sweetheart, this is life. Not war." Mom cups my cheek. "We don't have enemies here."

That's what she thinks. Everyone's fighting a battle or a war. Which means there's always a winner and a loser. And I don't plan on coming out the loser.

"Just give her a chance," Dad says, after drinking a couple of gulps from his mug. "Her contract is only for this Fall. If November rolls around, and you still don't like her, then we don't have to renew the contract."

That's the problem. I'm afraid I am going to start liking her. Not because she's good at her job, but because she can fill out a pair of jeans.

"It just seems to me that if you want to build a legacy, you wouldn't spend a chunk of our income on another full-time employee," I say. "Do we know that she has any experience with produce? Apples are pretty different from investment portfolios."

"Yes, they are. It's a good thing I have experience with both."

My spine tingles and my shoulders tense. I turn slowly and come face to face with Olive. If she's irritated by what she's just heard, she doesn't let on. Instead, she has a bright smile plastered on her lips. My stomach twists. With long, light brown hair swept into a low ponytail and a pair of green eyes the same color of the Green Mountains in summer, she has one of those faces you'll never forget once you've seen it.

At least I'll never forget it. I could live to be a hundred, and I'll always remember those full lips and her smooth skin.

I shift, suddenly more than a little uncomfortable in my jeans.

"Mr. and Mrs. Ferguson, it's wonderful to meet you in person." Olive gives my parents her attention. "I hope you don't mind that I just came inside. I knocked but—"

"Of course we don't mind," my mom says, wiping her hands on a dishtowel. She moves around the island to throw her arms around Olive like she's a long lost family member and not an employee. "Hunter was just telling us you'd arrived. I'm sorry we left you out there."

"There are worse places to wait." Olive's grin softens. "Your home and land are beautiful."

"We're pretty proud of them," Dad says, arriving at Mom's side to shake Olive's hand. "I suppose one of us should show you where you'll be staying—"

"I'll take her to the cottage." I blurt the words out without thinking.

A flicker of surprise flashes on Dad's face while Mom bites back a smile. Dismissing them both, I reach for the handle on Olive's suitcase. Our knuckles slide against each other and I still. A jolt of electricity shoots through me.

Hell, this is going to be a big problem. How am I supposed to get this woman to leave me—and my land— alone when all I want to do is make her stay?

THREE

OLIVE

I fall into step beside Hunter as he leads me to the cottage. The lodging is part of my compensation while I'm here. As he throws open the door, I gasp for the second time this afternoon.

"I know it's probably not as fancy as your place in New York," he says. "But it's been updated in the past year."

"It's perfect. Who lives here normally?"

"It's where I stayed when I was home on leave."

My gut sinks. "You were probably planning to live here before I came, right?"

He shrugs. "I can always build another place."

Well, now I feel bad. We make quick work of carrying my things inside. Hunter seems surprised that I don't have more.

"Would it be okay if I toured the property?" I ask. "If you can point me toward a map, I can guide myself."

He frowns. "You don't want to get settled in first?"

"Are you kidding? I've been dreaming about this place for a month now. I can't wait to see all of it."

"I can show you around."

"Oh, I don't want to be a bother—"

"I said I'd show you around."

He doesn't have to sound so happy about it. But, deciding it's better not to ruffle any more feathers than I have by merely existing, I fall into step beside him. As we walk the property, he points out key buildings.

"When we open for the Applejack festival next week, this place can get pretty packed," he says at the bakery.

"Have you thought about expanding?"

"It's in my three-year plan."

Of course, it is.

Then, he points to a cluster of trees on top of a hill. "We planted those a couple of years ago. It'll double our capacity within the next five years."

Camera raised to snap a photo of the young trees, I turn to ask him a question, but trip over a rotting apple. I fly forward. He catches me before I fall. We stand, frozen in place for a moment. His hands grip onto me tightly, and my belly flutters.

"What did I tell you about walking and being on your phone at the same time?"

I clench my eyes shut. "I swear, I'm not just here to take pictures." Though, based on the fact that my clumsiness has gotten the best of me twice now while doing just that, I can't blame him for not believing me. "It's just so beautiful here."

He shakes his head, and I sigh. I guess I'll have to prove I'm more than a ditz with a camera phone.

Helping me to stand upright, I tuck my phone in my back pocket as if to say 'look, I can be without my phone.' With a sigh of his own, he shoves his hands in his pocket.

"Are you thirsty?" he asks.

HUNTER

I turn to Olive carrying two piping hot cups of apple cider. "Let's drink these over on that picnic bench."

She accepts the cup and sips. "Oh, this is delicious."

"There's plenty more where that came from."

"Is this made from apples here in your orchard?" she asks, taking a seat.

"Of course." Then I run through the process of what apples we use to make products—like cider and apple doughnuts to sell—and which ones we leave for guests to pick. As I run through the line-up of our products, she occasionally interrupts me with surprisingly insightful questions.

"You seem surprised by my questions," she says eventually.

I might as well come clean. "I am a little. You've clearly done your research."

"I have." Annoyance flickers in her eyes. "I didn't just see a bunch of pretty pictures and come here to live my best Fall. I came here to work."

"Why?"

"It's hard to explain. But, I guess the TL:DR"—whatever the heck that means—"I've spent so much of my life having to bust my butt to meet other people's expectations. I've been competing against people for everything. First place in class. Getting an internship. Heck, even winning a ribbon for best Jack-o-lantern at my parents' country club. None of it was for the journey or the experience. It felt so fake. I just wanted to be part of something real. I wanted to be part of something that sang to my soul."

My throat clogs as I hear the emotion—the passion—in her voice. I feel an overwhelming desire to pull her into my arms and kiss the breath out of her.

And, I feel like a dick for being a jerk to her.

I swallow hard. "Do you think this place will sing to your soul?"

"I hope it will." She sets her cider down and meets my stare dead on. "I'm here to pull my weight. I'm here to do whatever I can to help take Ferguson Family Orchard to the next level. I'm willing to do the work and prove myself to all of you."

Again, I feel like a real dick.

"We started off on the wrong foot." I scratch the back of my head. "I'll admit, I didn't want you coming here." Before she can interrupt, I cover her hand. I try to ignore the jolt of lust that flashes into the pit of my belly. "It's not personal. I just didn't think we needed the help."

"So why did your parents hire me?"

"I think they're worried about me."

"Why?"

I sigh again. "As I'm sure they've told you, up until two months ago, I was a Navy Seal." When her eyes widen, I nod. "I always planned on coming back here to run the orchard. But I'd guess my parents want to make sure I'm not jumping back into civilian life too soon."

"So I'm a contingency plan?"

"I think I'm more of the contingency plan." My lips curve into a half-smile. "Whatever their reasoning, it looks like we're both in this for the long haul. Truce?"

I offer her my hand. She takes it and gives it a shake. Again, I try to ignore the tug in my belly from the feel of her palm against mine.

"What else would you like to see?" I ask, drawing my hand back.

"Everything."

"Could you be more specific?"

She purses her lips. "I have heard that your apple doughnuts are amazing."

"Would you like to learn to make them?"

"Really?" She pulls a face. "I should probably confess, I'm a terrible cook."

"There are no terrible cooks, just people who haven't learned how to cook properly yet."

"Did you just make that up?"

"No. My mom did." I grin. "Meet me at the bakery at five o'clock sharp tomorrow."

"In the morning?"

"Unless you can't handle an early wake-up call."

Her eyes narrow. "Oh, I can handle it."

Something tells me she can and she will. And, damn, if I don't admire that about her.

FOUR

OLIVE

I watch Hunter closely as he rolls out the dough and cuts perfect circles.

"What's that called?" I ask, pointing at the tool in his hand.

He holds it up. "This thing?"

I nod.

"It's a pretty fancy tool. I'm not sure you can handle it."

My eyes narrow. "I think I can handle it."

"This"—he wiggles it in my face—"is called a doughnut cutter."

I stop mixing another batch of dough and stare at him blankly. "Are you serious? That's all?"

"Think you can keep up?"

I roll my eyes and go back to mixing the flour while he explains the rest of the recipe. We've been at this for a couple of hours already. When I arrived promptly at five this morning, I caught a mix of surprise and admiration on his face. As if he assumed I'd miss the early morning call time, but was secretly pleased I hadn't.

Taking advantage of his seemingly good nature, I run a few of my ideas for the Applejack festival by him. He listens while I list off a few of the short-term plans that we can easily put in place before opening next week.

Pausing in his work, he looks at me. "How do you know so much about all of this?"

"My grandpa owned a small orchard in New Hampshire. It wasn't anywhere near this size though."

Hunter arches an eyebrow. "I didn't realize your family has an orchard."

"We don't anymore. My parents sold it." My heart clenches at that. "All my dad ever saw with that property was dollar signs."

"What did you see?"

"The happiest memories of my childhood." I turn back to the dough, rolling it out the way I watched Hunter do it just a few minutes ago. "I begged my parents to keep the place. I told them we could run it. I kept a journal of all of my ideas."

It's a journal that's sitting on the counter just a couple of feet away from us now.

"Why didn't they listen?"

"I was ten." I give a humorless laugh. "I guess I can't really blame them for ignoring the pleas of a child."

"So that's why you wanted to work here?"

I glance up to answer but find myself grinning instead. "You have some flour on your nose."

He swipes at it, adding more flour in the process. "Did I get it?"

"Not even a little." Chuckling, I lean up to wipe it away. As I do, he captures my wrist in his hand. My breath catches in my throat. My gaze drops to his lips.

I don't know who moves first. But in a flash, our arms are around each other, and his lips are on mine. I kiss him hungrily, poring all the frustration of the past couple of days into the kiss. Somewhere, in the back of my head, I know this is a bad idea.

But I tell that voice to shut up, as I open my lips to his tongue. He slides his hand down the curves of my body. His thumb traces the sides of my breast, and I gasp as it moves lower and lower. He grabs my ass, pulling me closer so I can feel the hardness of his desire against my belly. I reach for the top button of his shirt when I hear a clatter behind my shoulder.

We jump apart and turn to find Mr. Ferguson standing in the doorway to the bakery.

"Your, uh, mom wanted me to come and see if you needed a hand with anything."

"I think we have things covered here," Hunter says, sparing me a quick glance.

My cheeks burn red as I turn back to the dough and roll like my life depends on it. After a few more awkward seconds, Mr. Ferguson leaves. Once we're alone, I release a breath with a shaky laugh.

"Whoops," I say.

"That's one way of putting it."

"It would probably be best if we made these doughnuts."

"Agreed."

I give a sigh. I tell myself it's in relief at Hunter's easy agreement. But deep down, I know that's a lie.

I waste no time laying out the issue when Laurel answers the phone. "I have a bit of a problem."

"Oh no!" She gives a gasp that puts the one I made the day before to shame. "Has the place turned out to be a roach motel? Are they trying to fire you?"

"What? No! Why would you think any of those things?"

"Because you said you had a problem."

"A bit of a problem," I remind her. I take a deep breath and get it out. "I think I have a crush on Hunter."

"The owners' son?"

"The very same." I launch into an explanation of all of our dealings from the moment I arrived. I don't hold anything back. Not even the part about how my toes curled in my boots when he kissed me.

Laurel releases a low whistle. "Remind me again of why this is a problem."

"Because I work with him."

"So? Workplace romances are super hot."

"But I'm trying to prove myself to him as a businesswoman."

"I don't know what to tell you other than to use a condom."

I roll my eyes. "Remind me why I bother calling you."

"Because you love me."

Heaven help me, I do. Just like I really, really like Hunter Ferguson. And as long as the air cracks between us whenever we're together, it's going to be a bit of a problem.

HUNTER

I'm refilling my water bottle when my dad enters the kitchen at the house. It's the first time I've seen him since this morning in the bakery. I have a pretty good feeling he's been dying to give me a little grief ever since.

He reaches for the coffee and fills his mug. "It looks like you and the new business development manager are getting along better today."

I sigh. "It was just a one-time thing."

"You don't owe me any explanations. But can I give you a piece of advice?"

"I'd rather you didn't."

"Well, tough. I'm your dear old dad. So humor me." He rests a hip against the counter and waits for me to face him. "Not many people know what you've been through during the past fifteen years."

My jaw hardens. "You know I can't talk about my missions."

"I know. Everything you did the last decade was classified." He studies me over the rim of his mug as he takes a gulp. "That had to be hard. Not having anyone you could confide in."

"I had my team."

"And you lost some of them."

My hand balls into a fist at my side. He's right. I have lost a number of my friends through the years. I've had experiences I wish I could erase from my mind. But I wouldn't give any of it up if I had a second chance. I served my country to the best of my ability. I gave all that I could. I have no regrets.

I swallow past a lump in my throat. "You said you had advice."

"For about half your life, you've had to keep things guarded for the safety of yourself and others. But now, you have a chance to set some roots. To share life with people."

"Right . . ."

"It's a good thing to set roots and to share your life." He cuffs my shoulder. "God knows I couldn't have made it without your mom. I'm not saying it's the same thing for you and Olive. Heck, you two just met. But if you care about her—if you think you could have a future—don't hold anything back."

"You sound like a greeting card," I quip. But, I hesitate a moment and throw an arm around him. "Thanks, Dad."

He gives me a squeeze back. "Now, it would appear Olive left a little something behind in the bakery this morning."

He hands me a small notebook. "Maybe you'd like to return it."

It's on the tip of my tongue to say I can give it to her tomorrow. Then I remember his advice. Don't hold back. Set roots. I still can't explain it, but I feel called to Olive. Why fight it?

Taking the notebook, I walk the short distance to the cottage. The whole way, I think about ways of inviting myself in for a conversation. But as I arrive, the front door flies open, smoke billows out. I race toward the door.

Olive appears with a dishrag in hand, shooing the smoke out.

"Is everything okay?" I ask, gripping her by the shoulder.

"Oh, I just burnt my dinner."

I sniff. "What were you cooking?"

"A frozen dinner."

"I think we can do better than that." Handing her the notebook, I throw open the windows on my way back toward the kitchen. There, in the open microwave, I find the offending dinner. "What was this?"

"Some sort of pasta dish."

Rolling my eyes, I look through the counters and find what I need. Some dried spaghetti. A couple of pots. A tomato and onion. I open the fridge and find fresh basil and garlic.

"It looks like my mom has been here to stock the kitchen."

"She has." Olive blows a lock of hair from her forehead. "Of course, it's mostly lost on me."

"Come here. I'll show you how to make your own pasta."

Pulling out the cutting board, I set the ingredients out and talk her through it. Though it takes a little more coaxing, Olive joins me in preparing the marinara sauce.

"Where'd you learn to cook like this?" She frowns in concentration as she makes precise cuts in the tomato. "In the military?"

"From my mom. She believed both of her children should be able to work their way around a kitchen."

"Just like your dad believed both of his children should be able to work all of the tools in an orchard?"

I grin. "You're a perceptive thing."

"I try to be." She glances up from the cutting board, her eyes sparkling. "That is why your parents hired me. Even if I might look and sound like a big city snob."

"I said I was sorry."

"And I said I forgave you. But I'm also stubborn, so I'll probably bring that up from time to time."

"Stubborn you say? I hadn't noticed."

She scoffs at that. As we continue to cook hip to hip, we talk about some of our favorite movies and songs. When I tell her I haven't heard of half the bands she mentions, Olive throws her hands up in mock disgust.

"You, sir, need a serious education. I'm going to have to make you a playlist."

"And, I suppose I'll have to be a gentleman and listen to it." Stirring the sauce on the stove, I lift the wooden spoon to my lips and nod in approval. I hold it out to Olive. "Come here. Try this sauce."

Her gaze meets mine. My stomach tightens as she moves toward me. Resting a hand on my arm, she leans up, arching her neck to sample the sauce.

"Mmm." She licks her lips. "That's good."

Then her gaze flickers to my mouth. Setting the spoon down, I flip the burner on the stove to Low. We can leave the sauce to simmer. But we can't leave this electricity between us alone.

"Olive?"

"Yes?"

"I'm going to kiss you now."

FIVE

OLIVE

Though he's given me fair warning of his intention, I still gasp when Hunter's lips meet mine. I instinctively snuggle closer to him, slipping my hands up his chest. His muscles contract under my fingertips, stirring the excitement brewing in my belly.

As our tongues meet, my toes curl in my boots again. God, how is this man so sexy? In two kisses, I feel like he's awakened something deep inside of me. Something desperate and urgent that needs to be released.

When we pull back, I'm pleased to find his chest is rising up and down every bit as quickly as mine.

"How long did you say that sauce needs to simmer?" I ask.

"It's on low. We could leave it for an hour or so."

"Mmm." I run my tongue over my bottom lip, already swollen from his mouth. "I know a couple of ways we could kill an hour."

"Scrabble?"

"That's one way." I almost choke on a giggle. Then I glide my hand down to his buckle. He sucks in a breath as I pause just above his hard bulge. "I was thinking of something a little more hands-on."

He nuzzles the side of my neck, sending goosebumps down my spine. "You lead the way, honey."

Though I nearly trip over my own feet twice on the way to the bedroom, neither of us seems to mind. We're too busy pulling each other's clothes off, leaving a trail behind us like Hansel and Gretel.

His mouth on mine again, Hunter fumbles for the light switch.

"You want the lights on?" I ask, unable to mask my surprise.

"I've been thinking about seeing your naked body from the moment we met." Passion flickers in his eyes. "I want to see all of you."

If possible, his lust only heightens my own. Taking his hand, I pull him to the bed. We fumble and kiss, each of us moving our hands over each other. We swallow each other's gasps and groans.

Hunter pulls away suddenly, moving between my thighs. I push myself up on my elbows in time to catch his dark head disappear between my thighs. I barely have time to prepare myself before I feel his hard, strong fingers and his mouth touch my most sensitive spot.

"Oh." I gasp out. I dig my fingers into the bedspread.

His tongue moves over my clit as his fingers slide into me, demonstrating what is yet to come when our bodies inevitably join together. My insides quiver as he expertly pleasures me. When the quivers grow into waves of ecstasy that consume my body, I collapse against the bed, calling out his name.

He doesn't relent until I'm replete and spent. Crawling up my body he leans on one side, he gently strokes my skin. When I have the strength to open my eyes, he gives me a lazy grin.

"We're not done, are we?" I ask.

Chuckling he leans forward for another kiss. "Not at all."

"I'm on the pill." I blurt out.

His mouth freezes just a breath away from mine. He swallows hard. "I had a clean bill of health the last time I went to the doctor. And I haven't been with anyone since."

"Same."

We reach for each other simultaneously, bringing our bodies together. This time when he kneels between me, he positions his thick cock at my entrance. He taps the head against me. I gasp in anticipation.

"Are you ready?" he asks.

I nod because I can't think of a polite way to ask him to please fuck me right now. He presses the tip of his dick inside of me. I draw my knees up, urging him on, stretching with his size. Once he's in me completely, Hunter rests his forehead against mine. I grab onto his ass and buck up against him, showing him what I want.

With a chuckle, he follows my lead. Pulling out, he thrusts back in. With each thrust, the wanting inside me grows. Our skin sheens with light sweat as we push each other toward the edge. My orgasm comes first, squeezing him. With a groan, he moves in and out of me twice more. Then he thrusts in with a shout, pouring himself into me.

I don't know how long we lie here, tangled up in each other. But after a few minutes, I lean up to sniff the air.

Hunter pushes himself up to look at me. "Problem?"

"I was just checking to make sure the sauce wasn't burning."

His lips curve up. "I'd say we still have a good half hour or so before it's done."

"Perfect. I know just what to do."

SIX

HUNTER

I hum along to the music playing in my headset while I move bales of hay. Olive made me the playlist a couple of days ago. And while I'm pretending to listen just to humor her, I have to admit, it's grown on me. Just like she has.

Since we turned our relationship from professional to personal a week ago, the mood between Olive and I has lightened considerably. Though we still bicker—or maybe it's banter—as we discuss plans, we seal each and every argument with a kiss. And, once or twice, a quickie behind a closed office door. And, not to brag, once under an apple tree after a particularly heated conversation about where we should put the hot cider stand.

While we haven't said anything to my parents, I suspect they've already figured it out. Dad smirks every time I mention one of Olive's business ideas. Mom just beams at me every time I fill the thermos with Olive's favorite coffee in the morning.

"Someone is in a good mood."

I nearly jump out of my work boots as I swivel to find my sister laughing at me. Tugging the earbuds away, I throw my arms around Sienna and pull her in for a bear hug.

"Hey, Kid." I give her an extra squeeze. "I didn't think you were going to get here until tomorrow."

"And miss even one second of the Applejack festival?" She pulls back to grin up. "Not on your life."

"Do Mom and Dad know you cut classes?"

"What Mom and Dad don't know won't hurt them."

Pulling apart, I sling an arm over her shoulder and turn to look at the small festival area we've set up.

"So, what do you think?"

"It's incredible." I hear the sincerity mixed with excitement in her voice. "You really pulled out all the stops this year. Is that a bounce house?"

"Yep, and we have a couple of other games for kids just behind it. We're also going to have a candy apple making station next to the doughnut cart."

Sienna shakes her head. "I knew you had big expansion plans, but this far exceeds my expectations. How'd you get it all together so fast?"

"I had help."

"The fancy pants MBA from New York?"

"She turned out not to be so bad."

Sienna pulls back to gape at me. "Oh my God. You like her."

I shrug. "Sure. She's actually been good to have around."

"No, no, no. I know that look on your face. I know that

tone of voice." A devious smile spreads across her face. "You *like*-like her. Like, you want to get busy with her."

I swallow hard but keep my mouth shut. Her eyes go wide.

"OMG! You've already gotten busy with her."

"Shh." I glance over my shoulder, hoping that the part-time workers didn't hear. Granted, they have probably caught on too, but I don't want to advertise it to the masses.

"Look at you." The grin on her face grows even brighter. "I didn't even know you could blush. How long has this been going on?"

"About a week," I say low. "But we're keeping it quiet."

"Why?" Her brows knit together. "You aren't embarrassed or anything are you?"

"Of course not. It's just new." I give her a stern look. "If I promise to let you have the first batch of doughnuts in the morning, will you keep a lid on this until the festival is over?"

"You always knew how to strike a hard bargain. But it's a deal." She leans against me. "It's just really nice to see you like this."

"Like what?"

"Happy." A hint of darkness flashes across her face. She knows better than to bring up my service. "You deserve your own happily ever after."

I mull over those words. My own happily ever after. I suppose that is where we're headed. Though Olive and I haven't put labels on our relationship, I know I've never felt this way about another person.

"Tell me about her," Sienna urges.

"Well . . ." Pulling away, I shove my hands in my pockets. "She's the smartest person I've ever met. Present company included."

"I'll let that jab slide because you're a man in love. What else?"

"She has a way of seeing things. Like, she can look out at a stretch of trees and empty land and imagine bigger and better." I give a short laugh. "I spent all of my years in the service thinking about all of the improvements we'd make on the land one day. But in two minutes, Olive can take those ideas and make them bigger and better than I ever imagined. Plus, she can figure out how to make them happen."

"She sounds incredible. I can't wait to meet her."

I swallow past a lump that's lodged in my throat. "She should be back from town any minute. She needed to get a few things at the store."

"Oh, she might be a while." Sienna pulls a face. "I just got a text from one of my friends that an out-of-towner got into an accident on Main Street. Everyone has kind of gathered around to watch while the doctor attends her."

My heart hitches. "An out-of-towner?"

"I guess she was trying to send a text message and one of her high-heeled boots caught on the pavers—"

"I've got to go." Panic slices through me.

Sienna's eyes widen. "What's wrong?"

"I'm pretty sure that out-of-towner is Olive."

I hope I'm wrong. But I won't feel okay until Olive is safe and in my arms.

SEVEN

OLIVE

Reaching for the door to leave the grocery store, I juggle the overflowing bags in my hands.

"Here, let me help you." A man, who appears to be in his early thirties, reaches for the handle.

"Thank you." It's strange to think that a couple of weeks ago, I would've shaken off the offer for assistance. But in the time I've been here in Vermont, I've learned a lesson or two. Like, it's okay to ask for a little help when you need it.

Hunter would be so proud of me and my stubborn streak.

"Where are you parked?" the young man asks. "You've got your hands pretty full there. I'd be happy to help you out."

"I did kind of overdo the shopping," I admit, gratefully handing him some of the bags. "I came to get pie ingredients and ended up buying the fixings to make dinner and breakfast . . ."

I trail off and grin thinking about the pie I'm going to attempt to bake for Hunter tonight. With the Ferguson Family Orchard Applejack event opening tomorrow, I thought I'd celebrate by baking his favorite dessert. His mother gave me a knowing grin when I asked for her pie recipe. I've probably given away the full extent of our relationship, but I'll worry about that later.

Right now, I just want to do my best to make Hunter a pie he won't forget. And, hopefully, it won't be memorable because I gave him food poisoning.

Of course, true to nature, I couldn't just leave it at baking a pie. Once I was in the store, I had visions of making him a romantic dinner of his favorite foods. There are steaks for the grill. Ingredients to make potatoes au gratin— assuming I can figure out how to make them. I bought all the fixing for loaded baked potatoes just in case I screw them up. Then, I figured we'd need ingredients to make a salad and a loaf of French Bread. On a whim, I picked up eggs and bacon for breakfast. Then wine and beer.

I didn't realize just how much I'd put in my cart until it was time to carry everything outside.

Oh, that reminds me. I need to send Laurel the directions to the orchard for when she drives up tomorrow. Shuffling a bag, I dig into my purse to pull out my cell phone. I just have my hands on it when my heel catches on a crack in the sidewalk. It all seems to happen in slow motion. My ankle twists. My body flies forward. A carton of eggs sails out from the top of the bag.

The eggs and I all land on the sidewalk with a loud thud. I'm still sitting there in shock when the young man is at my side.

"Did you hit your head?" he asks.

"I don't think so." I start to move but wince. "I think I might have twisted my ankle."

"Do you mind if I check?"

"By all means."

Of course, half the town is now standing around us whispering and buzzing. A couple of squirrels are happily playing in the broken eggs. Great. Now, for the rest of my life, I'm going to be remembered as the woman who took a spill on Main Street.

"It looks like it's a sprain. But we should probably call the doctor to take a look," my new friend says.

"Oh, I don't know if that's necessary . . ."

"She's just across the street."

Twenty minutes later, a doctor is wrapping my ankle. My cheeks burn bright red, even though most of the crowd has disappeared by now. The helpful stranger—who I've now learned is Weston, a neighbor to the Ferguson's—got someone to clean up the broken eggs and he brought me a fresh batch.

So, really, all in all, it could be worse. I just have to think about how I'm going to tell Hunter and his family that I'm going to be on crutches for our opening weekend. I guess I really did make a lasting impression.

It's through this that I hear a familiar voice pushing through the remnants of the crowd.

"Crap." I clench my eyes shut and take a few deep

breaths through my nose before opening them to find Hunter crouched at my side.

"Are you okay?" He slips an arm around his shoulder and pulls me gently to his chest. "I came as soon as I heard."

"You were right. These high-heeled boots and cell phones don't mix. It's just a sprain, but now I'll be pretty much worthless for the rest of Applejack."

"I don't care about that. I just want you to be okay."

I pull back to gaze up into his eyes, and I see it. Worry. Care. Maybe even love. All of those possibilities clutch at my heart, filling me with warmth.

"I'm okay. Your neighbor Weston was being so helpful." I lean forward, lowering my voice. "You know he has a pumpkin patch, right?"

"Of course I do. His family has been my family's neighbor for over a century."

"And you share a pretty good fence line."

"Right. That bit of land had been a point of contention between our grandfathers."

I frown. "I was told that had mostly boiled over by the time anyone in your generation was old enough to pay attention to it."

"It has. But where are you going with this?"

"I'm just thinking. Especially because it sounds like there's a third neighbor who grows corn."

Hunter shakes his head, still not catching on. I suppose I can cut him a little slack. He does seem pretty frazzled by my brush with disaster.

Maybe I should try another approach. "Isn't it quite a

coincidence that three Fall-focused businesses all meet in one corner of land?"

A spark of understanding lights those dark brown eyes of his. "I don't know if I'd call it a coincidence."

"Oh, come on!" I roll my eyes heavenward. "We both know that bit of land would be a perfect place for a cross-sectional, cooperative festival. A place where all three families could come together and have a big Autumn hoopla where people from all over the region could come to live their best Fall life."

His lip twitches. "Best Fall life, hmm?"

"We'll work on the tagline."

He reaches out to brush loose strands of hair away from my cheek. The gesture is so impossibly sweet, I lose a bit of my annoyance. "I'm hoping you and I will have plenty of future Falls to go over all of these plans of yours."

My belly flutters. "Do you now?"

He nods. "Many, many future Falls."

"How many?"

"All of them." He rests his forehead against mine. "You see, it would appear that you aren't the only one falling head over heels."

"Wait. Are you saying . . ." My heart skips a beat. I swallow hard, trying to keep my emotions in check. "Are you saying . . . ?"

"Am I saying that I've fallen in love with you? Damn straight I am."

A giggle bubbles out of me as a tear slips down my cheek. "Well, I guess I love you too."

"Hmm. That doesn't sound very convincing. Put that

on the list of things we'll work on for the next fifty Applejacks."

"I don't know," I tease. "We have a pretty long list already."

"I think we're up to the task." He strokes my cheek and I lean into it. "Don't you?"

"Oh, definitely."

Because if I've learned anything this past week, it's that Hunter has a work ethic that matches mine. Which is to say, it's crazy good. I also know first hand that when we both put our whole hearts into something, there's nothing we can't accomplish.

It's safe to say we'll both put our whole hearts into building a life together.

EPILOGUE

HUNTER

"Higher, Daddy! Lift me higher!"

"Your wish is my command." I raise my four-year-old daughter up so she can reach another branch on the apple tree. "Your wish is always my command."

My wife grins from where she's spreading out a quilt for our picnic. With our two-year-old son helping her set out lunch, Olive and I are both at the mercy of our children's whims. 'Daddy, higher.' 'Mommy, a bug.' 'No, not that apple, Daddy.' 'No carrots, Mommy.'

It does beg the question of who exactly is in charge here. I know it isn't me. And, believe it or not, I've never been happier to follow someone else's command.

It's only fitting that our children would keep me on my toes when their mother has been doing that since the moment she arrived on my family's orchard. I should say our family's orchard. Olive and I got married over Christmas that first year. By the next autumn, my parents handed the reins to Ferguson Family Orchard over to us so they could retire. Of course, in their book, retirement means spoiling their grandchildren full-time.

Not that Olive and I are complaining. Fall gets busier every year. Olive's idea to create a partnership with the local pumpkin patch and corn maze has grown into a full-fledged fall festival. It takes over the whole town. People come from all over New England weekend after weekend to live their best falls.

At least, that's how Olive describes it.

That's not to say it's all been smooth sailing. In our nearly five years of marriage, we've been known to have the occasional spat that ends in a doughnut fight. There has been more than one occasion in which one or both of us has had to take a walk through the orchard to cool off.

But, we're equally good at making up. We're even better at making time for each other. Which is why we're here, the day before our apple-picking season officially opens. This was another of my wife's brilliant ideas. Every year, on the afternoon before the festival, we take off the afternoon for a picnic. It's a chance to appreciate the hard work we've done to prepare for the season. It's a chance to be present and enjoy the moment. It's a chance to celebrate the life we've made together.

"I think that's enough apples," I say, throwing my daughter over my shoulder. She kicks her legs against my chest while she giggles. "We'd better leave some for our customers."

"And you'd better get here before we eat all of the cheese," Olive calls out.

Settling on the blanket, I press a kiss to Olive's lips.

Our daughter makes a gagging face. That only encourages me to plant a louder, noisier kiss on her mother's lips.

"You've always been a contrary man," Olive says when I pull back. "And I love you for it."

I give her another peck, my heart brimming for this woman and the family we've made together. Then we turn our attention to our children and lunch and living our best Falls.

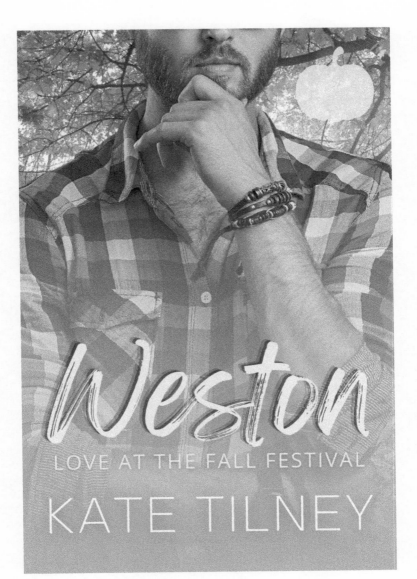

Weston

LOVE AT THE FALL FESTIVAL

KATE TILNEY

ONE

SIENNA

Stepping out onto the front porch of my family home, I take a deep breath. Filling my lungs with the fresh mountain air, I feel more like myself than I have in a while.

"It's good to be home."

"Who are you talking to?" My brother, Hunter, asks as he bounds up the steps. "Not your cup of coffee, I hope."

"Would it be a problem if I was?" I raise the mug to my nose and breathe in the heavenly aroma. "I'm practically in a relationship with this cup of Joe. There is nothing in the world that feels as good as the first sip of coffee in the morning."

"Clearly, you and that pretty city boy aren't doing it right if you think coffee is better than sex."

I nearly choke on my coffee. Hunter slaps me—hard—on the back until I'm breathing properly again.

When I am, I glare at him. "You ruined my first sip."

"It was worth it to see your face."

"I am your baby sister. What would Mom say if she heard you talking to me like that?"

Now it's his turn to frown. He shakes a finger at me. "If you tell Mom about this, I'll tell her who really scuffed up the wood floors in the living room."

I clamp my mouth shut. It's been fifteen years since I tried out my new pair of roller skates in the living room. In my defense, they were a Christmas present and there was eighteen inches of snow outside. And, I was only six. I was impatient.

Mom had freaked out when she saw the scuff marks. In a true moment of sibling solidarity, Hunter had sworn the marks came when my cousins moved the table so there was more room to open presents.

I've been in my brother's debt ever since. Damn.

"Fine. I won't tattle." I take a proper sip of coffee and savor it an extra moment longer to make up for the last spoiled drink. "Kevin and I broke up, by the way."

The taunting smirk slips away from my brother's face. In its place, there's genuine sympathy.

"I'm sorry to hear that." He slings an arm over my shoulder. "Are you okay?"

"I'll be fine. It's been a couple of weeks, and I'm pretty much over it."

For the most part, I mean that. While Kevin and I had dated since my sophomore year, a lot of the initial attraction that brought us together disappeared. And crude as my brother was with his remarks, he wasn't totally wrong. For the last few months, there just wasn't anything happening between us—in or out of bed.

And when Kevin suggested I drop a few pounds—and

maybe that it would help our sex life—I'd kicked him out of my apartment and my life.

"Are you sure?" Hunter asks.

"Positive."

"Good. Because once you finish that cup of coffee, I need you at the festival grounds." His grin is back. "And if you want to be a hero, you'll bring a thermos of that coffee with you."

"Is the baby keeping you up?" My little niece was born just last month. Already, she has me completely wrapped around her finger. If she's keeping my brother up at all hours, I like her even more. He deserves to lose a little sleep after all the trouble he's given me through the years.

"She's an angel." Hunter masks a yawn with the back of his hand. "But my wife had me up late redoing the tables in the bakery."

"Remind me to send Olive a pie later."

Hunter nudges me in the side. "I'll see you at the festival grounds soon."

Though I wouldn't mind spending the whole morning here on the porch with my coffee, I finish the mug in a couple of drinks. Pulling on my work boots, I fill a thermos with more fresh-brewed coffee and start my walk toward the festival grounds.

Ferguson Family Orchard has been part of our history for generations. Fall has obviously always been our busiest time of the year. But while business stayed steady, the costs of operating the orchard rose faster than we could keep up. That was why our parents hired Olive to join us last year. In just one year, she's grown our business and added new revenue streams for the off-season.

But this fall, we're launching her biggest project yet. We're partnering with two of our neighbors, who run a pumpkin patch and corn maze respectively, for an inaugural Green Mountain Valley Fall Festival. Basically, we'll do everything we've done in the past but bigger and together. There will be more activities. More games. And more city visitors, which means more money for all of us. The town has been buzzing about the festival since January. I'll admit, I'm just as excited to see how it's going to turn out.

Making a quick pit stop at the bakery to pick-up a box of apple cider doughnuts, I arrive at the entrance of the festival grounds just as the first visitors are pouring through the gates.

"I'm so glad you're here." Olive, my new sister-in-law, flashes me a warm smile as she throws her arms around me. Then she sniffs the air. "And you brought doughnuts."

"And coffee." I hold up the thermos.

"Bless you." And, if I'm not mistaken, tears actually fill Olive's eyes. "I can only have one cup because I'm breastfeeding. But that first sip is the best part of my day."

"Ah-ha!" I pump a hand in the air victoriously. "You make sure to tell your husband you said that."

Olive nods in bemusement as I pour her a cup and she takes a doughnut. I leave one of each for my mean big brother. Then, I offer one to Weston, one of the owners of the pumpkin patch.

As he faces me, my breath catches in my throat. Was he always so tall? And were his shoulders always this broad? When he takes the offered treats, I can't help but notice how the flannel of his shirt stretches over his muscular chest.

"Thanks." He flashes me a quick grin, the light reaches his dark brown eyes. My heart pounds a little bit faster.

I swallow hard and take a doughnut for myself—more as a distraction than out of hunger. I chew thoughtfully on my first bite, barely tasting the savoring mix of flavors. Instead, my attention is focused on how thick the dark hair poking out from under Weston's cap looks. And how his jaw is so strong. I swear, I've known him my whole life. But was Weston always this good looking?

Someone calls my name, pulling my attention away. I nearly choke on the doughnut in my mouth when my gaze lands on the person calling for me. Weston thumps me on a back just like my brother did half an hour ago. And just like my brother, it's less help than he probably thinks.

When I finally have my breath, I croak out the surprise visitor's name. "Kevin."

My ex dares to flash me a perfect smile while his arm is slung around a beautiful young woman.

"Sienna, I'd like to introduce you to my girlfriend, Alexis."

"It's a pleasure to meet you." Psych. Weston's hand freezes on my back even as my blood runs cold. "You never expressed any interest in coming to see my family's orchard before."

"Yes, well, I was telling Alexis all about it, and she just had to see it for herself."

"This place is charming AF." Alexis holds up her bedazzled smartphone. "My Insta followers are going to go crazy about this place."

"I hope this isn't weird for you," Kevin says.

"Why would it be weird for me?"

"You know, because of our history. And I've moved on."

I set my coffee and doughnut on the table, as an idea pops into my head. It's crazy, but there's no avoiding it. "Oh, I've moved on."

Kevin frowns. "You have."

"Yep." I slide an arm around Weston, who stiffens. "This is my boyfriend, Weston." Then, imitating Alexis's voice. "Isn't he cute AF?"

TWO

WESTON

My tongue nearly rolls out of my mouth with Sienna's announcement. I'm about to ask if she's lost her damn mind when she rests a palm on my chest. Then, I forget to think about anything.

As my libido kicks into overdrive, I try to pay attention to the exchange going on between Sienna and her ex-boyfriend. The dude and his new lady look like they just stepped out of a magazine spread for over-priced outdoor gear.

"I had no idea you were dating someone already." The way Kevin says it makes me want to smack him upside the head.

"Why should that surprise you?" Sienna looks up at me with pure adoration on her face. For a second, I forget that this isn't real. That whatever she's trying to pull is an act. "Weston and I have known each other for years. We reconnected a few weeks ago. Sparks flew. It's like we were made for each other. Isn't that right, Puddin'?"

Puddin'?

"Like a fairy tale." I slide my hand from her back to her side. Then I tug her close and she starts in surprise. "Speaking of fairy tales, Dumplin' I need to tell you a story. In private."

Not waiting for a response, I turn around, taking her with me. Olive Ferguson watches us, mouth open wide as I guide Sienna into a trailer that is serving as our communal war room for the festival. I have more than a few questions for this young woman. More than a few things to say. I give her a light push inside before slamming the door shut.

Fortunately, no one else is in here. Good. I'd rather not have an audience for this. Gripping her shoulders, I bring her to face me. I'm ready to lay into her when the look on her face gives me pause.

She throws up her hands against my chest. "I can explain."

It takes me a second to respond. I release my hold and shove my hands in my pockets, taking a step back. "Then start explaining."

"So that was Kevin, my ex-boyfriend."

"I remember him." I narrow my eyes. "Wasn't he the dude who ordered a steak at the diner and sent it back because he didn't like the cut?"

"That was Kevin." She pulls a face. "Look, believe me when I say I know he's a Grade A piece of crap. That's why I need your help. Please, will you please, just go along with this whole boyfriend-girlfriend thing while they're here?"

"I just don't get it." I shake my head, because it doesn't make sense. "The guy is a tool. Why does it matter if you're single or in a relationship?"

"Because . . ." She throws her hands up in frustration and starts pacing the length of the narrow room. "Did you get a look at his new girlfriend?"

"Yeah." I lift a shoulder. "She seemed okay."

"Okay?" Sienna spins on her heel to glare at me. "She's gorgeous. Like she stepped out of a magazine."

"She's not prettier than you if that's what's bothering you."

Sienna opens her mouth—probably to protest—but clamps it shut. She stares at me, her green eyes wild. Everything about her is wild right now. The dark, messy curls piled on top of her head. The way her full breasts are rising up and down with her unsuppressed anger—or frustration. I can't quite tell.

Then, Sienna shakes her head and continues. "Without getting into too many details, let's just say my size was a factor when Kevin and I broke up."

"Your size?" My eyebrows knit together as I glance over her curvy figure with appreciation. I swallow hard as I imagine feeling them pressed up against me. Hell, I can't imagine any red-blooded man who wouldn't want to bury himself between her thighs.

"And just a few weeks after we break up, he shows up with a woman who probably has a cover deal with a fitness magazine."

Now, what she's saying starts to make more sense. My fist clench into balls in my pockets. That ex of hers isn't just a tool. He's a God-damned idiot. And I wouldn't mind letting him know just what I think about him.

Sighing, I unclench my fists and ease my stance. "You really think having a fake boyfriend will help?"

"At the very least it will keep him from talking shit about me when we get back to campus." She shrugs. "It's my last year of school. I just want to get through it with some dignity intact."

"Does anyone who's gone to at least one party in college get through the whole experience with their dignity intact?"

She grins then, and I feel like I can breathe again. I hadn't realized how much the tension in her face and in her body was feeding my own.

"Would you please just do this for me?" Her tone is so sincere, so hopeful, it grips my heart. "I'll help at the patch all week."

I can already feel my reservations crumbling. But I can't resist asking, "What if we don't need help at the patch?"

"My sister-in-law told me that your right-hand man is in bed with two broken legs this week." She grips her hands together and holds them up, as if in prayer. "Please do me this solid."

She's right. I am without my foreman after he took a stumble off a ladder. My parents and I can manage without him, but it would be nice to have the extra help.

Plus, she's staring at me with those wild, hopeful eyes. Hell. I'm never going to be able to say no now.

Heaving a sigh, I pull off my hat to scratch the back of my head. "I guess I have one question for you."

"What's that?"

"What on Earth does 'AF' mean?"

Sienna's eyebrows relax and a slow grin spreads across her face. "Sometimes I forget how old you and my brother are."

"That doesn't answer the question."

"No, I guess it doesn't." The smile on her face widens. "AF is short for 'As Fuck.'"

"'As fuck,'" I repeat, stroking my chin thoughtfully. "Do you really think I'm cute as fuck?"

Now she rolls her eyes. "That sounds like a conversation for another time. In case you've forgotten, we have a fall festival to help run."

"Oh, I'd never forget that. Especially not since I just landed myself an extra pair of hands." A pair of hands I wouldn't mind seeing splayed across my body. Clenching my jaw, I clear my throat, trying to dismiss the thought from my head. Instead, I hold out my hand. "You have yourself one boyfriend for the week."

Here's hoping I don't live to regret this.

THREE

SIENNA

My eyes narrow into slits when Kevin and his Instagram perfect girlfriend enter the barn for pumpkin painting later that day.

"Easy, Tiger." Weston squeezes my shoulders. A tickle of delight runs down my spine. I know he's just trying to show support—and play the part of the doting boyfriend. But is it bad if I kind of like it, too? "Don't forget they're paying customers."

"And don't forget they're jackasses." I frown. "At least Kevin is. I don't know enough about Ms. Influencer to say if she is."

"I think we have our answer."

Alexis makes Kevin walk in with her two more times—lips pouting and arm extended out to apparently capture the perfect shot—before she's satisfied.

"Yeah. It's probably safe to say she's a bit of a jackass."

Weston squeezes my shoulders once again before releasing them. "But they're paying customers."

"I know, I know." I sigh. "And the customer is always right."

"I never said that. But we should at least let them blow a chunk of change before we give them hell." Weston winks at me before leaving to help another customer select a pumpkin for the challenge.

This time, my belly flutters a little. Okay, I know this is only for sure. That he's doing me a huge solid by playing along so I don't look like a pathetic loser in front of my ex. But my goodness, is Weston sexy? Did they put something in the water while I was away at school for the past six weeks? Or have I really been blind to how well he fills out a pair of jeans?

"Umm, excuse me." Alexis waves me down. "Ma'am."

"Did she seriously just ma'am me?" I mutter under my breath. With a sigh, I drag myself away from my gorgeous view and make my way across the room. I pull a tight smile. "May I help you? Ma'am?"

"This green is too putrid." She wrinkles her nose. "Do you have something in more of a Granny Smith shade?"

"We have all of our paint varieties out," Weston says, coming to my side. "Honey, what do you say we show Miss Alexis here how pumpkin painting is done?"

Butterflies flutter in my stomach as he wiggles his eyebrows at me and flashes a toothpaste-ad quality smile.

"Sure. Why not?"

He helps me sit down, and my fingers tingle where he held them as he helped me into a seat. Who knew Weston was so chivalrous?

While we paint our pumpkin, Weston and I discuss some of our favorite movies and shows.

"You're a *Stranger Things* fan?" I pull back in surprise to gape at him. "No way. That's my favorite show."

"Same here." He holds up his hand for a high-five. "Up top."

Laughing, I slap his hand. He closes his fingers over mine before I can pull back. He lifts our linked hands to his lips and gives them a kiss. My pulse quickens. Dang. He's really good at putting on a show. I don't think anyone would guess that we're not a real couple.

Swallowing, I take a deep breath to hopefully settle my nerves.

"Did you always know you were going to take over the pumpkin patch when your parents retired?" I hope the change in subject will be enough to keep me from thinking about how much I'd like to feel those lips of his on every inch of my body.

"You mean if they retire?" He shakes his head as he leans over me to clean his brush out in the water. "Like your parents, they might claim to be retired, but they're always underfoot."

"Still, did you want to come back and do this or did it feel like something you had to do?"

"You mean the way Archer feels?"

I nod, thinking about our third partner in this fall festival. While Weston and his family had jumped at the chance to collaborate for a fall festival, Archer had held off for a while. It seems, Archer was thinking about selling the place to a real estate developer.

At the last minute, he changed his mind and kept the land and joined the party.

I wonder if leaving has ever crossed Weston's mind.

"My parents never pressured me into taking over," Weston says slowly like he's choosing his words carefully. "They've only ever wanted me to be happy."

"And does being here make you happy?"

"It's in my blood. All of this"—he gestures out the barn door to the people eating slices of pie on picnic blankets, taking photos at the stands, and carrying their bags of apples with pumpkins tucked under their elbows—"it's as much a part of who I am as the color of my eyes or the way I wear my hair."

The passion for all of this is clear, and it warms my heart. "It's in my blood, too."

"I never had a doubt. It's just too bad your brother is such a jackass. He'd make your life hell if his wife wasn't around to keep him in check." There's no heat in his words and a sparkle in his eyes, so I know he's just having a little fun at my brother's expense.

"Did you ever wish you had siblings?"

"Yeah." He pulls a face. "My folks don't talk about it. Still, I know they tried for another kid. For a while, they were looking into adoption but that fell through."

My gut twists. "That had to be hard for them."

"I'm sure it was." He pulls a tight-lipped grin. "I think it's one of those things that can either drive a couple apart or make them stronger."

"And your parents."

"Strong as a rock." He shakes his head at himself. "Because of their issues with infertility, my mom has never pushed me to get married and have kids. But that hasn't kept her from dropping hints."

"Do you want to have kids?"

"For sure. If I find the right woman, I'd want to do it all. Build a house. Grow this business and land. Have a few kids."

The vision of a few mini versions of Weston running around makes me feel a little tingly. So does the thought of a 'right woman.' I brush a strand of hair away from my cheek, wondering what kind of a woman she might be. Wouldn't it be something if she turned out to be me?

He flips his pumpkin around to face me, interrupting my thoughts. "What do you think?"

On his pumpkin, he's painted the ugliest monster I've ever seen. "I love it."

Across the table, Alexis rolls her eyes and mutters to Kevin that, "Some people have no taste."

He leans forward to look at mine but pauses. "You have some paint on your cheek."

Reaching out, he wipes it aside with his thumb. My breath catches as his warm, calloused skin moves over my cheek. Our gazes meet, and if I'm not mistaken, interest lights his eyes too.

Then he drops his hand to the side and clears his throat. "I should probably go see if anyone needs help."

When he leaves, I release a breath I hadn't realized I was holding. And as I take a few breaths, one fact becomes abundantly clear. I have a huge crush on Weston. And that could really make this fake relationship of ours even more complicated.

FOUR

WESTON

Sienna's ex is a real piece of work. After spending part of the past twenty-four hours with him, I wonder what she ever saw in a guy like Kevin. Like his girlfriend, he seems to be all about appearances. Sienna isn't like that. She's so laid back. So comfortable. So authentic.

Kevin, on the other hand, is a giant tool.

I'm almost surprised when the wonder-couple shows up for the pie-eating contest.

"Aren't they afraid they'll get their clothes dirty?" I ask Sienna as we set out the last of the pies. "Didn't Alexis say they were both wearing outfits from her sponsors?"

"Maybe she has an affiliate deal with a company that does spot cleaning or sells laundry detergent." Sienna and I share a grin. "Besides, Kevin is so competitive. He'd never give up a chance to try to prove he's hot shit."

We split up to pour water glasses for the competitors as the happy couple finds a spot at the table lined with pies.

Kevin takes a seat while Alexis stands behind him. She's live-streaming on whatever social platform she's using today.

I set a glass of water in front of Kevin a little harder than necessary. "Are you ready to go, Champ?"

"Not as ready as some people. It's a good thing Sienna isn't competing." He smirks. "That girl always has had an appetite, if you know what I mean."

My jaw clenches. Oh, hell no. Sienna must have been playing down just how big of a dick he'd been about her gorgeous curves. I will not stand for it.

"I have no idea what you're talking about."

Kevin, at least, has the good grace to flush a little around the collar of his overly starched shirt.

"Forget it." He tugs at his collar. "Let's just say I feel pretty good about my odds."

"Sounds like you could use a little more competition." I shouldn't do this. It crosses the lines of professionalism, no doubt. But after his comment about Sienna, I just can't let it go. "How would you feel about going up against an expert?"

He smirks. "Are you proposing a challenge."

"I might be."

"I'm in." Kevin claps his hands together. "Babe, did you hear that?"

Alexis turns away from her camera phone. "What's that, Babe?"

Gag me.

"I'm taking on pumpkin boy, here in a one-on-one pie-eating contest."

"Ooh, it's a pie-off!" Alexis winks at her phone. "Who

do you think will win? My super sexy boyfriend or one of the owners of this pumpkin patch? Comment with your guess. And don't forget to 'like' and 'subscribe' to my page so you can watch it all go down."

People around us scramble as they arrange a new table with only two place settings. Sienna joins me. Oh, man. She's probably going to try to talk me out of this. It's not only unprofessional, but it's downright petty.

"Did I hear right?" she asks. "You're going head-to-head with Kevin?"

I nod, swallowing hard.

She rests a hand on my shoulder and leans up on her toes to whisper in my ear. "Show him no mercy."

She kisses my cheek, sending a jolt of lust straight to my dick.

As we take our new seats, Kevin extends his hand. "May the best man win."

"He will." I release his hand.

Hunter—who has been hanging around the patch more since his sister filled him in on our arrangement—stands on the other end of the table.

"Ladies and gentlemen, we have a real treat for you," he says. "Before we begin our official pumpkin pie eating contest, we have a sidebar competition."

He introduces us both to great applause. "Gentlemen, are you ready."

At our nod, he starts the timer. "On your mark. Get set. GO!"

Hands behind our backs, Kevin and I lean forward to start on the pie. I drown at the cheers around us, only vaguely aware of Sienna standing across from me, shouting words of encouragement.

As I take bite after bite, ignoring the churning in my stomach, I see Alexis move from side to side of the table, recording every minute.

Hunter starts the final countdown of ten seconds. I only have a bite or two to go. Though my stomach protests, I think about seeing the grin fall off of Kevin's face when I'm declared the victor with half of his pie still fully intact. Powering through, I clear the plate.

"Time!" Hunter reaches for my arm and holds it high in the air. "We have a winner."

The look of defeat on Kevin's face is even better than I imagined. Alexis pouts for the camera. Fighting back my own grin, I turn to Sienna. She jumps up and down clapping as I push myself up from the table. It takes all my willpower not to groan. And when I reach her, she throws her arms around my shoulders.

"You did it! You slaughtered him."

My hands instinctively go around her waist. "Well, I've had my share of pumpkin pie through the years."

"Just take the compliment. You're my hero." She leans up to press a light kiss to my lips.

Before she can move back, my hold on her tightens. The churning of pumpkin custard leaves my stomach, and it's replaced by something else. Something more all-consuming. Something more intense, more serious. My mouth moves against hers and she tenses for a second. But then she relaxes, angling her head to grant me more access.

This is only a performance. We're just pretending to be

a couple. Even as I repeat those words in my head, my body ignores them.

When her lips part to mine, my tongue swoops in. She groans and my grip tightens on the back of her shirt. The sound of her brother chuckling over my shoulder reminds me that we're not alone. Regretfully, I break off the kiss. But I keep my gaze on her beautiful face. When her eyelids flutter open, we share a grin.

"You guys might want to tone it down a little," Hunter says, clamping me on the shoulder. "I know you're trying to suck it to numbnuts over there, but we have children in attendance."

"We'll be more G-Rated next time."

Sienna snickers at that. I know she thinks I'm making a joke. But I'm serious. I know there will be a next time. I'd set my watch to it.

FIVE

SIENNA

As we set out for the evening hayride, my patience is wearing thin. Kevin and Alexis are cuddled up together on the wagon, wrapped in an oversized flannel blanket from a brand Alexis keeps mentioning in all the videos she's shooting for her "peeps."

We're only twenty minutes into the two-hour ride that will take us through all three properties, and I'm trying my best to remember the breathing techniques I learned during a Mindful Meditation seminar I took one semester on a lark.

It's been like this all weekend.

You'd think with three whole properties for them to visit, I could maybe get a break from their public love session. Thank goodness for Weston, is all I can say. Not only has he played the part of doting boyfriend to perfection, but he's also turned out to be a good buddy.

He's also become a frequent guest star in my dreams. Ones that have made me blush when I see him for the first time every morning.

We go over a bump in the road, Alexis squeals and grips onto Kevin.

"OMG, peeps." She giggles into her phone screen. "This place is, like, so rustic. Can you even?"

Gritting my teeth, I lean over to Weston, who is seated next to me, steering the open-top truck. "Am I being overly sensitive, or is Alexis obnoxious?"

He chuckles and slides an arm over my shoulders. "I'd like to toss the pair of them over the side. But it probably wouldn't help our Yelp rating."

I snort and cover my mouth in horror. Eyes wide, I pray that Weston didn't hear me. But based on the loud guffaw he just made, that's a prayer that will go unanswered.

Sitting back in my seat, I try my best to ignore our only passengers. Instead, I study Weston. He really has been the best all week. He's had my back at every turn. And watching him give Kevin a sound butt-kicking at the pie-eating contest will go down as one of the greatest moments in my memory.

"I really appreciate your doing this," I say, low enough that our passengers won't hear.

"Hey, I'm getting free labor."

"Yeah, but that's fleeting." I hesitate a moment before placing my hand on his arm. "What you're doing is helping me save face. And that will last a lifetime."

"It's been a pleasure."

And the way he says it, I almost believe it. Just like I almost believe he enjoyed the kiss we shared yesterday at the pie-eating contest as much as I did. No, I'm not going to sell myself short there. I could tell he enjoyed that kiss as much as I did. Heck, in the end, he was the one kissing the daylights out of me.

I fan myself with my hand because it suddenly feels hot in this Autumn air.

"Are you okay?" Weston asks, slowing the engine. "Because I have some water in the cooler if you want."

Before I can reply, Alexis screams. Weston slams on the brakes and we turn to find her having a complete and total meltdown that would put a toddler to shame.

"What's wrong?" I call out.

"There's"—sob—"a"—sob—"bug!"

"Oh, you've got to be kidding me," Weston mutters, reaching for the ignition.

"Babe, just calm down." Kevin rests his hands on her shoulders. "It's just a beetle."

"Don't you dare tell me to calm down." She pushes his hands off of her shoulders and jabs a finger in his chest. "The only reason I agreed to come to this place was that you wanted to rub it in that girl's face. But I'm done pretending this is fun."

"But babe—"

"No way." She hops off of the back of the trailer and wipes the hay off of her. "I'm going back."

"We can drive you," Weston calls out.

But she doesn't turn around. Swearing under his breath, Kevin jumps out of the trailer and races after her.

Neither Weston nor I say anything for a couple of minutes as we stare after them.

"Well that was something," he says at last.

"You can say that again."

"Do you think we should go find them?"

I shake my head. "I have a better idea. They paid for a private hayride, right?"

"That's right."

"Then let's hang out a while."

Weston flashes me a grin. "I like the sounds of that."

He drives us to the top of a hill that overlooks the apple orchard and pumpkin patch. Opening the picnic basket that Kevin and Alexis had bought and left behind, we have a meal of turkey and cranberry sandwiches and slices of pumpkin pie. While we eat, we talk about nothing and everything.

As Weston polishes off his pie, I notice he has a crumb on his lip. Without thinking, I reach out to brush it away. It's like the other day painting pumpkins. The electricity. The heat between us. Only this time, we don't have an audience.

We fall together, mouths colliding and teeth scraping as the sexual tension between us erupts. As his fingers fumble with the buttons of my chambray shirt. When he pulls it over my shoulders, his hands greedily cover my breasts.

"God, I've been thinking about these for days," he says, tearing his mouth from mine. He makes quick work of removing my bra and sending it the way of my shirt.

We land on the straw and I wince. Weston leans up on his elbows.

"Are you okay?" he asks.

"Fine." I grit my teeth. "I've forgotten how uncomfortable hay is on bare skin."

He looks around us, his gaze lingering a little longer on my full chest, before nodding. "Give me one minute."

He disappears and returns a moment later. Offering his hand, he helps me sit up as he spreads a large flannel blanket over the hay.

"Your ex's girlfriend left this behind." Leaning back on his heels, he gives me an apologetic look. "I know flannel can get a bit scratchy, too, but hopefully it feels better."

"I like the flannel." I lean back on the blanket. Already it feels a million times more comfortable. I reach for him, and he covers my body.

Lowering his head, his mouth comes around one of the nipples and he sucks it into his hot mouth. I buck up again, my fingers sliding into his hair, urging him on. His free hand continues to rove my body, lowering to the top of my jeans. While he pleasures my breasts, he flips open the button and slides his hand under the denim and my panties.

"God, you're wet." His breath tickles my breasts.

"It's what you do to me."

He groans in response as his fingers find me. I gasp, my body all sensation. It sings like it never has before. Like no one has ever known how to touch me before. Faster than I could ever imagine possible, I feel the desire swelling in my belly. Growing until it consumes every inch of my body.

Weston doesn't let up the teasing and stroking until the last ripple of ecstasy passes. I've never come so fast or so hard. No man has ever had this effect on me.

And we aren't done.

We cast aside the rest of our clothing and come together again. Limbs tangling as well as our mouths and tongues. Our hands caress and explore. There's no holding back. His hard length presses against my bare belly, exciting me once again.

"I need you to be inside of me."

He rests his forehead against mine. "Let me grab a condom."

I grip his arm before he can move.

"I'm on the pill. And I just had a trip to the doctor last week."

It had seemed like a good idea after I heard Kevin had a girlfriend already. I push that thought out of my head. I don't want to think about him now. I don't want him to spoil this moment.

Weston grins. "Clean as a whistle here."

"Good." I buck up against him, and he lets out a low chuckle as he lines up at my entrance and thrusts in. "Oh!"

He stills. "Are you okay?"

"Don't stop!" I move again, grabbing onto his bare ass, digging my fingers into him. Urging him on. "Take me."

And he does just that. Stroke after stroke. We capture each other's gasps and moans with kisses and words of praise and endearment.

When I feel that familiar tug again, I call out his name, squeezing him.

With a final thrust and grunt, Weston releases inside of me. We collapse against the flannel and hay, wrapped in each other.

We lay there for minutes, maybe hours, as the dusk

turns to night, and the stars light the sky. When I see one fly by I make a wish. I wish that this moment means our relationship has gone from fake to real. And I wish it will last forever.

SIX

WESTON

There's a little more pep in my step when I walk out to the patch the next morning. And, hell, the fact that I'm using phrases like 'pep in my step' speaks volumes. After a week pretending to be with Sienna—and a night really being with her— I'm a goner. Hook, line, and sinker, I'm falling for this girl. And, son of a bitch, I'm even whistling while I work.

In my defense, it's impossible not to think about her. I am freshening up the hay on the trailer where we spent a satisfying couple of hours under the stars. It's only natural I'd think about her and what happened. And about how much I look forward to a repeat performance tonight.

It's funny how fast things can change. I've spent the last few years thinking it might just be me and my family's land. After never feeling anything more than attraction to a handful of women over the years, and never finding someone who wants to share in this dream of mine, I got used to the idea that maybe I'd never find my forever woman. I was fine with that. At least, I told myself I was. Now, Sienna has me looking at life in a whole new way. It's a life of fewer what ifs and more whens.

Who would have guessed the woman of my dreams has been the girl next door all these years?

I reach for another bail of hay and the whistle dies on my lips. Striding my way is the one person who can sour my mood. Kevin. Only, this time he's without his Insta-gram-perfect girlfriend.

"Where's your better half?" I ask.

"She's headed back to Boston." Kevin shoves his hands in his pockets and looks over my shoulder. "Have you seen Sienna around?"

"Not since this morning. In bed." I add because I'm petty enough to want to see his reaction to that statement.

It has the desired effect when Kevin pulls his lips into a tight line.

"I can give her a message if you like," I offer.

"What I have to say is a little more personal than that." He squirms a little under my stare. "Alexis dumped me, okay. I was hoping Sienna might give me a ride to campus when she heads back tomorrow."

It takes all my willpower not to show my surprise. Or to chuck a bail of hay at his head. Instead, I take a moment to channel the anger flowing through my veins.

"I'll give her the message." My jaw ticks. "If you'll excuse me, I have some work to do."

I wait until he's just out of distance before I grab the bail of hay and throw it on the wagon. Unfortunately, it's too soft to be gratifying. So I pick up another and another, gritting my teeth while I plaster the trailer with hay. It's my own fault. I knew this was only temporary. It was only supposed to last while she was in town and only to prove a point.

But now that the point no longer needs proving—and with only one more day before she heads back to school—it will all be over.

I shout as I throw in the next pack of hay, wishing I could ease some of this anger.

"Whoa!" With the baby strapped to her chest in one of those carrier things, Olive cautiously comes to stand next to me. "Was that Kevin?"

I almost ask her if she has eyes, but I don't. It's not fair to snap at her. She's not the reason I'm angry.

"That was Kevin."

"Where's that girlfriend of his?"

"Back in Boston." I kick the dirt with my boot. "They broke up."

"So much for a romantic lovers' week in the mountains." Olive's eyes narrow. "If the fancy girlfriend is gone, why is he still here?"

"Based on the questions he was just asking? I'd say he's hoping for another chance with Sienna."

Olive's eyes widen. The baby stirs awake, and Olive rubs her back, gently soothing her while she thinks.

"And how do you feel about Sienna?" she asks at last.

"I shouldn't feel anything."

"I didn't ask how you should feel. I ask how you do."

I consider walking away. But I'm a man who doesn't run from his problems. Besides, in the last year, I've gotten to know Olive pretty well. She's not the kind of woman who gives up easily. If I don't answer her now, she'll just keep pestering me until I do.

Sighing, I shove my hands in my pocket. "Sienna makes me feel . . ."

"Happy?" Olive offers when I can't finish the sentence. "Content? Excited? Love?"

"All of those things." Because now it all seems so clear. "Sienna makes me feel. Period."

"That's a good thing." When I shake my head, she frowns. "Why isn't it a good thing?"

"Because this is only supposed to be temporary. Now that wonder boy is single again, I have no doubt Sienna will be ready to call things off."

Olive's eyebrows knit together. "You've been spending quite a bit of time with Sienna the past couple of days, haven't you?"

"Sure, I guess."

"And in that time, has she ever given any indication that she's stupid?"

"None at all." My tone takes on a hard edge. "In fact, she's one of the smartest people I know."

"And don't you think she might be too smart to get back together with a guy who made her miserable? Especially when she's been spending time with a guy who makes her happy?"

"Do you think I make her happy?"

"I know you do." Before I can protest, Olive grabs my arm. She holds it until I make eye contact. "Sienna is my sister now. And in the year I've known her—which included part of her relationship with Kevin—I have never seen her smile so much or so genuinely."

I don't say anything. I just don't have the words. But I like the idea of being the reason Sienna smiles. I'd like it more if I could be the reason she smiles for the rest of her life.

SEVEN

SIENNA

My brother slams a crate of pumpkins on the counter and I jump.

"Holy crap!" I pull the earbud out of my ear and turn off the music playing on my phone. "What are you trying to do? Give me a heart attack?"

"You seem awfully jumpy and distracted there, Sis," Hunter smirks, and I'd like to wipe it off his face. Maybe by pulling his hair like I did when I was little. "Doesn't have anything to do with the fact that you were out all night does it?"

"Of course not. I was listening to music."

"You were having a dance party in the barn."

"So what if I was?" I shove the earbuds in his face before tucking them into my pocket for safekeeping. "I'm in a good mood."

"Someone must have discovered there is something that feels better than coffee after all."

I roll my eyes because that's what little sisters do when their brothers make gross jokes. But I don't disagree with him. He's right. Last night, what happened between Weston and I was better than the first sip of coffee in the morning. And I don't say that lightly.

Plus, there's more. On a very basic level, Weston and I understand each other. He seems to like me for me. He doesn't think I need to be thinner or wear dressier clothes. He doesn't want me to leave this land that I love so much.

This may have started out as an arrangement to help me save face. But the feelings I have are real. But one night of passion doesn't mean we're on the same page. I sigh.

Hunter's brows come together. "What's wrong?"

"I'm really starting to like Weston."

"He's a good guy. You're good together."

"But this is supposed to be temporary."

"All of this is temporary." Hunter gestures around us. "The leaves change color and fall to the ground. In the spring they come back green. Then they do it all over again."

I shake my head. "What are you getting at?"

"Just that nothing stays the same forever. And sometimes, the most beautiful things grow out of nothing."

I blink. "When did you get so poetic?"

"Love does that to a man." Then a pained expression crosses his face. "Ah, hell, your ex is coming. I'm glad you kicked his ass to the curb. He's the worst."

Groaning, I turn and give a half-hearted wave to Kevin. "Can I help you?"

"Hey." He kicks the ground with his over-priced shoes. "Could we talk in private?"

"I'd rather we didn't."

Annoyance flickers on his face and looks at my brother. Instead of leaving, Hunter stays in place, folding his arms across his chest.

"Fine. We'll do this here." Sighing, Kevin runs a hand through his hair. "I was a dick. I see that now."

"Right." He'll get no arguments from me there. "With you so far."

"And I was hoping you might forgive me."

Now it's my turn to sigh. "There's nothing to forgive. As I said, we just weren't right together."

"Do you think we could be friends?"

Again, I'd rather not. But I suppose there's no harm in burying the hatchet. "Sure. We can be friends."

Relief crosses his face. Maybe I've judged him wrong. Maybe he isn't the selfish, egotistical man I always found him to be. Maybe it's like I said: we just aren't compatible romantically.

I'm about to offer to shake his hand when he says, "Could you by any chance give me a ride back to campus? Alexis ditched me here."

Suddenly the olive branch makes sense. I take a step toward him, ready to tell him he can hitchhike when I hear Weston call my name. Forgetting about Kevin for the moment I turn as he crosses the path. My heart leaps. I wonder if it will always do that for him. I wonder how I couldn't have seen before that he's the perfect man for me.

When he reaches us, Weston glares at Kevin before facing me. "You guys aren't getting back together, are you?"

"Ew. Gross." I shake my head. "Not even a little. Not ever."

"Good." He releases a shaky breath. "Because that would really get in the way of what I'm about to say next."

His gaze meets mine, and the look I see in it makes my heart pound harder and faster. "I'm ready for whatever you say."

"Sienna Ferguson, the past few days have been the most fun I've had in years. And I don't want them to end." He takes my hand in his and holds them to his chest. "Will you go on a date with me? I mean, a real one?"

I hear Kevin suck in a breath over my shoulder. "What do you mean go on a date? Weren't you dating already?"

"Aw, shut up dude," Hunter says. "Come on. Let's leave these two alone. I'll help you book a ticket on a Greyhound back to Boston."

"A bus!" the horror in Kevin's voice almost makes me smile.

And I do smile, but it isn't for him. It's for one man. Only one man. I squeeze Weston's hands. "I'd love to go on a real date with you."

The brightest smile I've ever seen crosses his face. "I figure I should take the woman I plan to spend the rest of my life with on a proper date."

My heart pounds even faster and joy radiates through every inch of my body. "I think that would be a good idea."

And then he pulls me into his arms and we kiss each other like there's no tomorrow. Only there is—a tomorrow filled with love and possibility and us. And every bit of the life we build together will be real.

EPILOGUE

FOUR YEARS LATER

WESTON

When I see Sienna round the corner of the barn with a wheelbarrow overflowing with pumpkins, I drop the bail of hay and intercept her.

"What do you think you're doing?" I take the handles from her. "Weren't you supposed to be helping your brother at the apple orchard today?"

"They're pretty much good to go. Hunter and Olive were just setting out for their traditional pre-festival picnic. Besides"—she flashes me a big grin and bats those bewitching eyes of hers—"I missed you."

Hell. How's a man supposed to argue with that? Releasing the wheelbarrow, I loop my arms around her and pull her close for a kiss. Though we've been married going on four years, nothing sets my pulse racing like this woman. No one stirs my soul. And no one drives me up the wall quite as she can.

I suppose that's what has made our life together so interesting.

When I break off the kiss, I rest my forehead against hers. She takes several deep breaths and grips onto my arms. I can't help but grin. It's good to know that I still have the same effect on her now that we're an old married couple.

After we 'made it official,' as Sienna likes to say, we did long-distance while she finished school. I was the loudest person cheering for her when she walked across the stage and accepted her diploma. A week later, we had a small wedding—just family and friends—on a stretch of land where our family properties meet. We built a house on the very spot. Our parents each gave us a chunk of land to make our own. We've done just that while working with our families to build up both properties.

But now that we're working on a very important collaborative project of our own, I'm keeping an extra watchful eye over my girl.

Which reminds me. "My mom might need help setting up the pumpkin painting."

Sienna pulls back to glare at me. "You know your mom won't let anyone else set up the paint supplies."

"You could check on the pies."

She rolls her eyes. "We both know the pies are baked and in the refrigerators waiting for the big day."

Dropping my hold on her, I pull off my cap and run my hands through my hair. Her expression softens then.

"Hey." She grabs my forearm and waits for me to meet her gaze. "The doctor said I'm good to do most of my regular activities."

"He said you shouldn't lift anything heavy."

"This isn't heavy."

Giving her a stern look, I turn to lift the handles on the wheelbarrow. "This is definitely more weight than any pregnant woman should be pushing around."

She sighs. "Fine. I won't push the wheelbarrow. But you have to give me something to do. I'm not going to spend the next six months doing nothing."

Setting the wheelbarrow back down I wrap my arms around her. It takes a moment, but she raises her arms to hug me back. I don't know how long we stand here holding each other, but I feel steadier when I speak next.

"We've been trying to have this baby for so long," I whisper. "I just don't want anything to happen."

"I promise, I'm going to take such good care of this baby." She leans back to cover her belly protectively. "But I need room to breathe."

"I'll give you room to breathe." I cover her hand with mine. "And I'll do my best to ease up. But I can't promise I won't worry."

"You're just being a good daddy and husband." She leans up to kiss my lightly whiskered chin. "That's part of why I love you so much."

"Not half as much as I love you both." Right here, standing in my arms and growing under my hand are the two most important things in the world. Seasons may change, but the love I have for them both will only grow.

Archer

LOVE AT THE FALL FESTIVAL

KATE TILNEY

ONE

LAUREL

The gravel road curves through a cornfield with rolling red and orange mountains in the distance. Unfortunately, I'm too busy paying attention to the conversation I'm having over the phone to appreciate the beautiful fall foliage passing by.

"Let's go over the checklist one more time," my best friend Olive says over the car's speaker. "I know, I know. You're a highly skilled professional, but this is my baby."

She's not talking about the baby she's carrying right now. The one that has her—under doctor's orders—on bed rest for the next few weeks. No, she's talking about the fall festival she established in a small Vermont town, somewhere in the foothills of the Green Mountains. The fall festival has built up her husband's family orchard business. And thanks to a collaboration with the neighboring pumpkin patch and corn maze, they've put their small town on the map.

That's the baby she's talking about. It's the reason I'm here, winding through backroads in the middle of nowhere. Hoping my car's GPS takes me to the Ferguson Family Orchard and not the town where *Children of the Corn* was set. Based on the rows and rows of corn stretched as far as the eye can see, that's looking more possible.

But it's the baby she's carrying that has me counting to ten so I don't tell her to shut up. Olive is not just my best friend. She's like my sister. And just like my sister, I love her and sometimes I want to pull out her hair.

"Let's go over the checklist," I say, trying not to let my annoyance through in my tone.

"Okay, first thing, after you're settled in, I've arranged for you to do a tour of the grounds with Hunter, Weston, and Archer."

"A tour with the property owners. Got it."

"With the festival opening in just one week, I want you to feel comfortable in any of our properties. The guys know you're supposed to have full access."

"How did the guys take the news that you were giving a complete stranger full access to their properties?"

She pauses just a moment too long with her answer.

"Oh my God!" I shout, slapping the steering wheel. "The guys are pissed."

"I wouldn't say pissed."

"Less than thrilled?"

She sighs. "That's a way to put it."

Less than thrilled. Pissed. Same difference. "And you're pitting me against them."

"Not against—with."

I'm about to argue with her, but I remember she's

carrying my next godchild. I count to ten and prompt her. "Back to the checklist."

"Tonight, I've arranged for the mayor to come over for dinner. My mother-in-law is cooking, so you can look forward to a good meal."

"Dinner with the mayor. Check."

From there, she runs through a long, long list of items that will have to be tackled before and during the list. I know them all by heart. Not only did she email me a copy of the list—three times—but we've also been over it by phone at least five times before.

I make the appropriate sounds as she goes through each item, taking the opportunity to survey my surroundings. It really is quite pretty here. Though I've always been more of a skyscrapers and coffeeshop on every corner kind of girl, I can appreciate the beauty nature is presenting before me. The trees are glorious shades of red, orange, and yellow. It's like something out of a painting.

I bet if I rolled down the window, I'd catch a whiff of a bonfire or maybe some of their famous apple cider doughnuts baking.

It's enough to almost make me understand why Olive gave up her luxurious city life for the rustic country. Almost.

From out of nowhere, a large object flies in front of me. It smashes into my windshield with a loud thud as I slam on the brakes. Sucking in a breath, my knuckles are white on the steering wheel. Eyes wide, I stare ahead trying to make sense of what exactly is staring at me. It's not quite human. Then again, it has a face. With eyes and a nose.

This is so *Children of the Corn*.

"Olive," I interrupt, my voice tense as I'm still not able to breathe. "I'm going to have to call you back."

I hang up before she can ask what's going on. Because I don't have answers. Not yet. Unbuckling my seatbelt, I throw open the door and slide out. Taking a deep breath, I straighten my spine. I step closer, reaching out a hand to pick up a pointy hat.

"Are you okay?"

Spinning on my high-heeled boots, I raise my fists, ready to face the intruder head-on.

A tall man in a red and black flannel shirt holds his hands up. "Whoa. I come in peace."

I keep my fists up. "Who are you?"

"I'm Archer. This is my land. And that"—he points at the figure on my windshield—"is my scarecrow."

"Scarecrow?" My hands fall to my side as I swivel back to investigate. Picking up the figure, with more confidence now, I hold it up and stare the straw-stuffed mannequin in the face. "Toto, I don't think we're in Boston anymore."

"Boston?" The man reaches my side and gives me a once over from head to toe. "You must be Olive's friend. Laurel?"

"I am. And you are?"

"Archer." He offers me his hand. His palm is rough and warm against mine. Electricity shoots through me. "As I said, this is my land."

"The corn maze owner." And now that I'm standing this close to him, I have to say. He's not bad on the eyes. With broad shoulders, a chiseled jaw, dark hair, and striking blue eyes, he definitely has a Prince Eric thing going for him. My belly flutters. I always did have a thing for Prince Eric. I hand him the scarecrow before I can do something stupid, like ask him to make out with me. "This is your friend?"

"Sorry about that. I was trying to hang it up—Olive's orders—and a gust of wind caught it." He squints his eyes. "Are you okay? Any damage to the car or you?"

"It'd take a lot more than that to scare me. I'm fine."

"Do you know where you're headed? Because I could ride along and show you the way."

I'm about to tell him that I can manage on my own. That I've been managing on my own for most of my life. But as I breathe in and catch a whiff of his musky scent, the prospect of spending a few more minutes in his company seems pretty appealing.

"That'd be great. Is your friend okay to ride in the back without a booster seat?"

He flashes me a bright smile that leaves me momentarily dazzled. Oh, the next couple of weeks might be more fun than I expected. I came here to help out my friend. But would there be any harm in sampling the local goods?

TWO

ARCHER

As Laurel reaches for the handle to the driver's side door, I flex my hand. It still tingles from when she shook it a moment ago.

There's something about this woman. Maybe it's the way she gaped at me with those rich, brown eyes when I told her I'd lost my scarecrow. Maybe it was the way she gave me—a stranger—just enough sass to be funny. Hell, maybe it's the way she's filling out that pair of jeans. Her hips are full, and right now she's giving me a prime view of her curvy ass. I flex my hand again, balling it into a fist.

Whatever it is about her, I've invited myself along to be her tour guide. She's only about a mile away from the orchard. I could have given her directions easily enough. As it is, I'll have to walk back here to get my truck. But I just knew I couldn't let her go. Not without spending a little more time with her. To see if what's pumping through my veins right now is pure lust or something more.

"So, you're from Boston," I say as I settle into the passenger seat of her four-door sedan. A car like this probably gets good mileage in the city. But out here, it'll wear down fast on all of our gravel roads.

"Born and raised." She flips on the ignition. "Have you lived here your whole life?"

"Most of it." I went away for college and worked in New York for a few years. But there's hardly any point in mentioning that now. Not when her full lips are pursed into a most appealing pout. "Olive says you have event planning experience."

"I do. I'm an event coordinator at a hotel."

"A lot of weddings."

"Only about a million of them." She flashes a grin and my pants grow suddenly tight. "Now, I've never thrown a fall festival, but it sounds like you have things under control."

"Olive sent you a copy of her checklist, right?"

We share pained looks.

"I'm glad to know I'm not the only one who got it. I swear, my phone almost caught on fire when I opened the email."

"I use my printed copy as a paperweight on my desk."

She chuckles. It's low and raspy. And sexy. I never knew you could describe a laugh that way.

I clear my throat. "Well, it's good to know we're in good hands."

"Oh, please. You guys could probably run this thing without me. Most of what I know about fall festivals I've learned from Pinterest and Hallmark movies."

My lips twitch. She is a sassy thing. And I like it. I like

a lot of things about her already. Those lips. Those eyes. Those out of control curves.

I shift in my seat to hide the tent my dicks about to pitch in my pants. "Well, we're glad to have you here to help out. This is only our second festival. And while Hunter, Weston, and I have a good handle on our own properties, it helps to have another person to keep us in line."

"I hope I'm helpful and not a pain in the ass."

"I doubt you're a pain in the ass."

"Want to bet?" She casts a sidelong glance, and I catch the sparkle in her eyes. "I just want to make sure Olive stays put in bed."

"We all do. I'm sure it breaks her heart to have to sit this festival out when she's put so much into building it."

"It does." She pulls her lips tight. "That's why I had to come help when she asked."

"She's lucky to have a friend like you."

"I'm the lucky one. She's always been such a good friend to me. It's the least I can do to pay her back." Her expression softens. "Plus, now I'll finally get the chance to 'live my best fall' as Olive likes to say."

"She does say that a lot." I shake my head. "But it's one hell of a good marketing campaign. It's kept this town hopping the past few autumns."

"So business is good."

"Business has never been better." It's going so well, we've caught the eye of some pretty big real estate developers. But, again, that's not a conversation for now. Especially not when it could put a damper on the fall festivities.

"What are you most excited to do for 'living your best fall'?"

She grins. "Well, obviously, I'm going to have to try every apple- or pumpkin-flavored food you have to offer."

"Sorry, not my department. I work mostly with corn."

"I've actually never been to a corn maze."

"Really?" I guess I don't know why that's surprising. "You don't get many corn mazes in Boston do you?"

"Not at all. How long have you guys done corn mazes?"

"My parents started it when I was a kid." Mentioning my folks makes my heart sink. "It's not what we're primarily in business to do, but it gives the farm a nice push at the end of the season."

"I don't suppose I could talk you into letting me try out the maze tomorrow."

"And stand in the way of living your best fall?" I fake scoff. "I could never do that. Olive wouldn't let me hear the end of it."

Plus, I wouldn't mind getting even more one-on-one time with this woman. Especially now that we're pulling up to Hunter and Olive's cottage at the orchard.

"How about I give you a tour of the grounds tomorrow?" I suggest.

"You know, that just so happens to be on Olive's checklist."

We exchange a grin, and my gut tightens. Yeah, I definitely want to spend a little more time with her. Though Laurel protests, I help her carry her things inside. Though she'll be here for a couple of weeks, she only has a couple of suitcases and bags. Most of the women I knew back in New York would've packed this much for a weekend away.

Hunter throws open the door and grins. "Finally. Now I can get my wife to stay in bed."

"Is she being a difficult patient?" Laurel asks.

"The worst."

"Hmm. I better go see her right away."

While Laurel goes in to find Olive, I motion for Hunter to follow me out onto the porch. His one-year-old daughter is in his arms and she squirms to be let down, and he obliges.

After Hunter closes the door behind us, he sighs. "That real estate developer has been in touch again, hasn't he?"

I nod, not asking how he knows. This is a small town. An even smaller community of landowners. Word gets around.

"So are you selling?"

I sigh. "I don't know. It's a really good offer."

"I can't tell you how to run your business, but we'd hate to see you go."

"You'd hate to see a swanky hotel go up on my property."

Hunter's lip twitches. "That too. But our families have worked side by side for generations. It would be the end of an era."

"I haven't decided anything yet." Which is the truth. This isn't the first offer I've had to sell, but it has been the best. "They're sending a rep out on the twelfth."

"That's the day after the festival starts."

"I think they want to see what you guys have built."

"What we've built," Hunter corrects. "You've put your heart and sweat into it too."

I've put my sweat into it. I don't know about my heart. And that is the problem. I just don't know if my heart is in this enough for the long haul.

THREE

LAUREL

I toss down an armful of towels when I reach the bedroom door and plant my fists on my hips. "What are you doing out of bed?"

Olive drops the binder in her hands and sinks back onto the bed. "I swear. I was only out of it for a minute."

"Am I going to have to tell Hunter on you? Again."

She pulls back the quilt and slides under. "I promise. I'll behave."

Rolling my eyes, I reach for the binder and hand it to her. "What's this?"

"It's some financial records." She sighs. "Archer has had an offer to sell his farm."

I arch an eyebrow. "I didn't know he had it on the market."

"He doesn't. But it's prime real estate. All of this is. We all get offers at least once a year."

But something about the way she says it makes me

think she doesn't feel as flippant about it as her words might suggest.

"Do you think he's going to sell?"

"I don't know." She shakes her head. "He came really close to selling a couple of years ago. But the harvest festival went so well, it seemed to change his mind."

"Hasn't the land been in his family forever?"

"It has. But everyone has their price."

"Even Hunter."

Olive rolls her eyes. "Okay, he, Sienna, and her husband are the exceptions to that rule."

"I wonder why Archer would be the odd man out in the group. Didn't they all grow up together?"

"They did, but your guess is as good as mine." Olive straightens the pages in her binder and sets it on her end table. "I've known the man a few years now. We've worked side by side. But we've never had a real conversation."

"Maybe he's shy." Though, I already know that isn't true. There didn't seem to be a shy bone in that handsome body of his when we met yesterday. "I can try to do a little fishing when he shows me around today."

"You must have a way with him." She shakes her head. "No offense, but I was pretty sure I was going to have to bribe him to get him to show you around."

"Why would you ever think that?" I wiggle my shoulders and fluff my hair, laying it on thick. "We both know I'm the cute one."

"And the humble one." She smiles then, and it's the first time I've really seen her at ease since I arrived. "I'm so glad you're here."

"I am too." I take her hand and give it a gentle squeeze.

"I wish it wouldn't have taken a medical emergency to get me here for one of your fall festivals."

"You have your own career."

"But this is such an important part of your life." I pat the back of your hand. "I'm glad I'm here now. Not just to help you. It's good for me to get away."

Her jaw drops. "Aren't you the one who said I was crazy to leave the city?"

"Oh, please. That was years ago." I roll my eyes, even as I fight back a grin. I did give her a hard time when she turned down a job with a Fortune 500 company to work on an apple orchard. But even though she's on bed rest, I've never seen her happier. This place—and the family she has here—really seems to suit her. "Besides, now that you're practically a local yourself, I can see you've found your place."

"And have you found yours?"

My stomach clenches. "Still looking."

"You know, the festival is getting big enough, we might need to hire some additional staff for next year."

"Don't get ahead of yourself." I squeeze her hand one more time before releasing it. "I told you this place is cute. I didn't say I was ready to sign a lease."

"Your loss."

The doorbell rings, and I instinctively fluff my hair again.

Olive's eyes go wide. "Oh my God."

"What?" I ask as I check my lipstick in the mirror.

"Do you have a crush on Archer?"

"Psh." I smack my lips, satisfied with this shade of red. In the mirror, I can still see Olive gaping at me. Oh, heck.

There's no point in holding back. "Fine. He's so sexy, my tummy gets a little fluttery."

"And what does he do to your parts south of the belly?"

"How can you ask such a thing?" I press my hand to my chest in mock surprise. "I'm a lady."

"That's not what you'll be saying in a couple of days." But Olive's eyes sparkle. "You're going to knock him dead, honey."

"I hope not." Because I'd like him very much alive for the fantasies I have involving him. What good is a sexy crush if he isn't living and breathing?

ARCHER

Laurel gasps and clutches my arm in a moment of fear as we turn the corner in the maze and come face to face with a monster.

"Holy crap!" She squeezes my arm tighter. "I thought corn mazes were for kids."

"They can be. This is the adult course."

"You couldn't have just made it triple-X rated with some nude magazines." She gives a shaky breath. "Sorry, I had no idea I was such a wuss."

"You're okay." Hell, having her soft body pressed up against me like this is better than okay. It's like something out of a wet dream. And I'm a grown man. I shouldn't be thinking about wet dreams. But she brought up porn. Still, it would be so easy to lean forward just another inch. Press my lips against hers. See if they feel—and taste—as good as they look. I'd bet my farm they do. "We could always bail out now and head for the kiddie corner."

"Are you kidding?" She loosens her grip on me and straightens her shoulders. "In case you haven't noticed, I am a confident, independent woman."

"I did notice." With her tits sticking out like that, it's impossible not to. "And I suppose a confident, independent woman like yourself never backs down from a challenge."

"Not in this lifetime."

She releases her hold on me and marches forward, letting out another gasp as she sees one of the zombies. Shaking my head, I follow her, a grin on my lips. She really is a joy to be around. During our earlier tour of the festival grounds, she proved herself to be more than capable of event management. She asked all the right questions—including some Hunter, Weston, and I hadn't considered. But the moment we left that behind to try out the maze, it's like she turned into a child again. She has so much excitement, so much enthusiasm for all of this, it's contagious.

Catching my stare, she waits for me to catch up with her.

"It must have been pretty fun growing up with a corn maze," she says.

"It had its moments. Mostly, it was a lot of work."

"So you didn't get a lot of time to enjoy the fun of the season?"

"Oh, we still had fun." I frown to myself. Though truth be told, I can't remember the last time I just wandered the grounds for fun. This is probably the first time since before I went away to college.

"What was your favorite fall activity growing up?"

I smirk. "What kind of question is that? Did you get it out of a magazine?"

"I'm just making conversation." She rolls her eyes and takes my arm again. My gut tightens and I cover her hand with mine. "Come on. Tell me."

"I guess I always liked having bonfires."

"I love bonfires." She gives my arm a gentle squeeze. "I can't remember the last time I had one."

"We'll have to set one up while you're here."

"I'll bring the s'more supplies."

"Now you're talking my language." I'm about to ask what her favorite fall activity is when something catches my eye and gives me pause. Not something—a lack of something. "Son of a . . ."

Her eyes go wide. "What's wrong?"

"It's the damn scarecrow."

She glances around us and shakes her head. "I don't see the scarecrow."

"Exactly." I stop myself just short of kicking the dirt in frustration. "I put it up last night and it's gone."

"Oh, shoot." She frowns. "Where could it have gone?"

"I don't know, but it's the third scarecrow I've lost this season."

Her jaw drops. "You have a thief?"

"So it would seem." Sighing, I run a hand through my hair. "We must have some kids stealing it as a prank. I have half a mind to start calling around."

"Why don't you?"

I shake my head. "I don't want to go accusing kids of wrongdoing when I don't have proof."

Laurel purses her lips. Some of the irritation eases out of my body as blood pools in my groin. Damn, but those lips could drive a man to distraction.

"I have an idea," she says at last.

I blink, twice, before her words register. "What's that?"

"We should hold a stakeout."

I arch an eyebrow. "A stakeout?"

She nods. "We can set up camp overnight nearby and wait to see if anyone comes to steal it."

"It's not a bad idea." I cast a glance her way. "Are you sure you're up for a night of roughing it?"

"Oh, please." She waves her hand at me. "You bring the firewood, I'll bring the s'mores."

I like this plan of hers more than I can say. Of course, I'll be a gentleman. I'll keep my hands to myself. But based on the way she's batting her eyes at me, I get a feeling I won't have to keep my hands to myself all night.

FOUR

LAUREL

Archer opens the passenger door of the truck and offers me his hand. I take it, enjoying the shiver of delight that runs down my spine at the contact.

"Thank you," I murmur.

"My pleasure." The way he says that last word gives me all kinds of ideas.

My eyebrows knit together as I glance around us. "Is this where your scarecrow attacked me yesterday?"

He chuckles at that. "It looks like the same spot, doesn't it?"

I nod.

"We're actually about half a mile away from the spot."

I shake my head. "I'm giving myself away as a true city girl, aren't I?"

"Most people wouldn't know the difference."

"But you do."

He lifts a shoulder as he pulls our supplies out of the

back of his truck. "It's my land. I guess if anyone is going to know it well, it should be me."

"You must really love this place."

He pauses a moment, a stricken expression crossing his face. "I guess it's like love. But it feels more like a sense of obligation. A sense of duty."

That's so different from how Olive's husband talks about the orchard. Or the way I heard Sienna and her husband, Weston, talk about their properties over dinner last night.

"A sense of duty," I repeat, hoping it's enough to keep him talking.

"My story starts off a lot like Hunter and Sienna and Weston." He hands me one of the sleeping bags while he sets up the tent. "We're all overseeing land that has been in our families for generations. We've all always known—in one way or another—that we would one day take the helm."

"But that doesn't mean it's what you want to do."

"Don't get me wrong. I'm proud of my family and all the work they did to build up the property through the years. They made it through tough times. Droughts. Depressions." He sighs, pausing in the middle of setting the stakes in the ground. "I just thought I'd have more time."

"Time for what?"

"Hunter served in the military. Sienna went to college. Weston never left, but he never wanted to." Archer leans back on his heels and stares at the corn. "I moved to New York after high school."

"I didn't know that." I sink to the ground next to him. "Did you go to school there?"

He nods. "I had a job. I planned to stay there until my parents retired. I figured I'd be in my thirties by then. I'd have my wild oats sown so to speak."

"What happened?" I ask when he falls silent.

"My parents were killed in a car accident when I was twenty-five."

My heart sinks. Instinctively, I reach out to cover his hand. "I'm so sorry."

"Thanks. It's been ten years, but I still miss them." He clears his throat. "I quit my job. Moved back. Took over. But my heart wasn't in it the way it was before. I don't know if it's because they're gone. I don't know if it's because I left part of myself back in the city."

"That had to be hard."

"It was." Sighing, he puts the last stake into place and stands. He offers me a hand and pulls me up. "It's not even that I miss the job. Or my place in New York."

"Maybe you miss the possibility of it all."

"That's exactly it." He gazes at me, intensity burning in his eyes. "Anyway, I guess that's why every couple of years I think about selling the place. Starting over somewhere else."

"You're talking about the offer from the developer."

He smirks. "Did Hunter tell you about that?"

"Olive did." I pull my lips together. "I don't blame you. It has to be hard to be here."

"It can be. It would be hard to leave too." He shakes his head. "I guess I'm looking for a reason to stay."

I gust of wind blows by, and I shiver.

"I should get a fire started." He piles the logs he brought. While he does that, I pull out the thick flannel blanket-scarf I brought and wrap myself in it. When he turns away from the fire, he grins. "You look all set for a bonfire."

"Don't you mean I look like I came out of a photoshoot for a bonfire?"

"That's not a bad thing. I'm not sure it'll keep you warm all night, though." He motions for me to move closer. When I do, he slides an arm over my shoulders. His body's warmth flows through me as we watch the flames flicker and dance. "How's this?"

I nod. "Perfect."

And it really is. The sun is setting. The fire is alive and warm. And I feel about as comfortable as I have in my life.

"This is nice." I regret the words almost the moment they're out of my lips. They're too mushy for a night of being on scarecrow watch.

But instead of rolling his eyes at me, Archer pulls me closer against the wall of his chest. The butterflies flutter in my belly as his warm breath tickles the side of my neck.

"It's very nice," he says.

ARCHER

The fire is crackling, and Laurel is cozied up to me when she straightens suddenly.

"I almost forgot?"

"What?" I ask, instead of telling her to forget about it so I can continue to keep her warm. It's been an hour since I bared my soul to her. I hadn't meant to spill my guts. But once it was all out, it felt good. Like a weight had been lifted off my shoulder.

And even though we come from such different backgrounds, somehow, we truly understand each other.

"I brought a little something for a night of camping." She holds up a tote bag. "S'more supplies."

My stomach growls at the word. "Oh, man. I can't remember the last time I had s'mores."

"The last time I had them, I was at sleepaway camp in middle school." She starts to unload the bag. "I couldn't resist."

My eyes go wide. "This looks like an awful lot of supplies to make s'mores."

"Let's just say, we're taking the standard and upping it a notch."

She hands me a pen that pulls out into a stake. "Whoa. That's clever."

"It's amazing what you can find during a little late night shopping." She hands me the bag of marshmallows and we each add a couple to our stakes. While the marshmallows roast, she explains the rest. "We have an assortment of chocolate-based candies and cookies. But I also brought along plane Hershey bars and graham crackers if you're afraid to be adventurous.

"I'm not afraid." To prove it, I use two M&M cookies and a peanut butter cup to assemble my sandwich. I take a bite and almost groan. "Okay. This is incredible. How'd you come up with all of this?"

She takes a bite of her own creation—snickerdoodles and a white chocolate bar—and her eyelids flutter in rapture before she answers. "Don't laugh. But I found this all on Pinterest."

I don't laugh, but I grin. "Why am I not surprised?"

She shrugs. "I can't seem to help myself. For years, I've been pinning all these ideas on how to live your best fall. So much that Olive has always teased me for it."

"Well it's nice you can put it to use now." I polish off the last bite of my s'more and reach for another marshmallow to make another. "This is probably a pretty different way of spending an evening than you're used to back in Boston."

She nods. "Very different."

"What does an ordinary weeknight look like for you?"

"Nothing Pinterest-worthy." She gives a humorless laugh. "Usually I stay late at the office. If I have energy, I make something quick for dinner. A few nights a week, I'm too tired and I pick up takeout. I fall asleep on the couch watching whatever true-crime series is new on Netflix."

"Sounds exciting."

"You have no idea." Her lips twitch with humor before her face sobers. "Honestly, it's pretty lonely. Ever since Olive left, it just hasn't been the same. It's weird to feel lonely when you're in a city with so many people."

"I get that. I felt the same way in New York. Hell, I had three roommates." I slide the toasted marshmallow onto a peanut butter cookie this time, covering it with a mini crunch bar and another cookie. "I was never alone. But I could still get lonely."

I bite into my s'more, and this time I do groan. "This really is fucking delicious."

"I'm glad you like it." She turns toward me, a grin on

her lips that grows wider. "Oh, you have some chocolate on your cheek."

She brushes it away and I lean into her touch. Her hand freezes in place as her gaze lifts to reach mine. The light from the fire dances in her rich, brown eyes. My self-control snaps.

We reach for each other at the same time. Lips collide. Breaths meet. The air between us sizzles and snaps, like the fire burning in front of us. As I slide my hand underneath her sweater, my body aching for her, I don't feel alone anymore.

FIVE

LAUREL

My fingers slide into Archer's dark hair. I part my lips, granting him more access. His hard hands slide under my sweater. I sigh into his mouth as they cup my breasts through the lace of my bra.

Following his lead, I unbutton his flannel shirt and slide it from his shoulders. I spread my fingers over his hot, hard muscles, marveling at how they ripple under my fingertips.

The rest of our clothes are soon discarded, and Archer lays me back gently on one of the unrolled sleeping bags.

"You okay?" He brushes a lock of hair away from my cheeks. It's so impossibly sweet, so tender, my heart swells.

I nod, swallowing hard against the lump in my throat.

Grinning, he lowers his head to capture one of my nipples with his lips. I arch up against him, gripping onto him as he nips and tugs, sending jolts of delight through me. He slides one hand lower until he reaches the part of my thighs. Gliding one long finger through the seam he groans.

"You're so wet," he says against my breast as he pushes another finger inside of me.

I buck up, gripping tighter to his shoulders as the pressure in my belly builds and grows. As he continues to work on my nipples and clit, the tension spreads until it's too much for my body to contain. With a cry, the orgasm rips through me, sending wave after wave of pleasure throughout me.

Still holding onto him, my breath comes in gasps as I push him onto his back.

"Now. It's. Your. Turn."

His chuckle turns into a groan as I grip his hard length, marveling at its size.

"I'm on the pill," I say quickly, ready to have him inside of me. "And I'm clean."

"So am I."

With that, I lean up over him and lower myself onto his cock. My lips part and I throw my head back in rapture as he fills me inch after delicious inch. His fingers dig into my hips. I press my hands flat on his chest for support. We stay frozen like that for one moment, each savoring the connection.

When my eyelids flutter open, I stare down at him. I catch the hunger in his eyes, as I push myself up so he can thrust into me. Again and again. Sweat sheens on our skin, glistening in the firelight.

I can feel the quickening in my belly again.

"Come for me," he moans. "Come for me, baby."

As if on command, I do. I call out his name as his grip tightens on me. He pushes in once more with a shout.

I collapse on his chest, which is rising up and down every bit as rapidly as mine.

"That was . . ." I shake my head. "There aren't enough words."

He cradles me closer, pressing his lips to my forehead. "No. There aren't."

We stare up at the sky, each of us gasping for breath. At this moment, I feel more whole and more complete than I ever knew possible. It's funny. I've always thought I was happy. Or at least content. I'd made my way in this world, and I didn't need anyone or anything to change that.

That was before. Now that I'm here, with Archer, staring up at the twinkling stars with a fire warming our bare skin, there's nowhere in the world I'd rather be.

A rustling nearby draws our attention.

"What is that?" I ask.

He shakes his head. "I don't know.

It grows louder and closer. We bolt up in unison. The top of my head smacks his chin and we both wince and mutter expletives as we grab for clothing. I button up his flannel shirt, trying not to enjoy the smell of his musk, as he tugs on his jeans.

"Where's it coming from?" I look around. "Do you see anything?"

He squints and his eyes go wide. "Oh my God."

"What? What is it?"

"The scarecrow." He points ahead. "Do you see it?"

I turn in time to see a group of four raccoons scurry up the pole. We stand in slack-jawed amazement as they make quick work of removing the scarecrow from the post and dragging it off with them.

"Should we go after them?" I ask when I finally find my words.

"What's the point? They're halfway to their lair." He starts to chuckle. His laugh grows fuller and louder as he swipes away at his face. "I've seen raccoons steal corn. I've seen them get into people's gardens. But what the heck do they want with a scarecrow?"

His laughter is so contagious, I'm beaming at him like a goof. "Your guess is as good as mine."

He shakes his head. "Should we head back home now that we've found the culprit?"

I almost say yes, but glancing around us at the camp we've laid out, this seems pretty perfect. "I'm game for a campout if you are."

He leans down to give me a quick kiss. "I have a few ideas for what we can do next with those s'mores."

SIX

ARCHER

Hot streams of water rain down on me, working out the aches and pains of the past week. But every single one of those aches and pains was worth it. We opened the fall festival successfully two days ago. And even Olive—when she'd received her report—had to admit, we'd done right by her.

The shower curtain slides open and I grin. Of course, so much of that success is courtesy of the outrageously brilliant and gorgeous woman stepping into the shower with me.

"Good morning, sweetheart." I pull her closer under the guise of helping to wash her back.

"Good morning," Her gaze flickers lower. "And good morning to you, too."

Her hand follows the trail of her eyes and she grips my already aching cock in her hand. The smile never leaves my face after that.

Once we've both found satisfaction, and washed our hair, we step out of the shower. I wrap a towel around her body, pulling her up against me as I meet her gaze in the bathroom mirror.

"There's a lot to be said for couples showers," I murmur against her ear.

She shimmies her shoulders even as she leans closer. "You're right. It's better for the environment."

"We both get hot water."

"It'll save you a fortune on the water bill."

My eyes darken. "And that's nothing to say about the personal satisfaction."

"Mmm. It is a good bonding experience." Her lips curve up, reminding me of how they felt wrapped around my dick just a few moments ago. "I mean, we've spent pretty much every waking—and non-waking—moment together the past week, but still."

"Very true." We have spent most of our time together since that night in the cornfield. We've worked side by side putting the finishing touches on the festival. We've had dinner at Hunter and Olive's every day. She's been here in my bed at night. In a day, I'd guess we spend about twenty-three hours in each other's presence.

It still doesn't seem like enough.

And at the end of this week, once the festival is over, she'll be headed back to Boston. We haven't talked about that yet, or what it will mean for us. But I know how I feel about her. I love her. She's it for me. Whatever it takes, I'm going to build my future with her.

I clear my throat. "I've been thinking."

"Oh, good. I'm glad one of us has been thinking. After

what you just did to me in the shower, I'm not sure I'll have a clear thought for at least another hour."

God, I love her. That love wraps around my heart, filling me with a joy I haven't had in a decade.

"Do you want to know what I've been thinking?"

"If it involves a second round in the bedroom, I suppose I'd be open for negotiations." She wiggles her eyebrows. "But we'll have to make it fast. We're due out on the festival grounds in an hour."

I start to tell her this isn't about another round. Though, now that she's brought it up, I might have to change my mind about that. But I'm distracted by what she's smearing on her face.

"What is that?"

"This?" She holds up the jar. When I nod, she grins. "It's a little face lotion I've been working on using ingredients from the farm."

I arch my eyebrows. "When have you had time to create an organic skincare line?"

"A lady always has her secrets."

My dick twitches at the way she says it. Yeah, I definitely think she's onto something with another quickie before we head out.

"What's in it?" As she lists off a bunch of ingredients, I shake my head in disbelief. "How did you even come up with all of that?"

Her lips twitch. "Pinterest."

Of course. "And does it work?"

"Stay tuned." She wiggles her eyebrows. "So, do you want to do it in here or—"

"Anywhere, but first, there's something I want to talk to

you about." I still her hands before she can distract me away completely from what I wanted to say. "I was thinking about next week."

She sobers instantly, and regret flickers in her eyes. If I had to guess, she's as bummed about the end of this week as I am.

I clear my throat again. "What if I came back to Boston with you?"

"For a visit?" Her face lights up. "That would be great. I could show you that cannoli place Olive and I were talking about."

"I was thinking of staying. For good."

Her jaw falls open. "But what about the farm?"

"There's a rep from the land developer coming today."

"You're going to sell?"

Even after all this time we've spent together, I can't tell if the shock in her voice is surprise or disapproval. "Your life is in Boston, right?"

"Yeah, I mean, I guess." She shakes your head. "But your life is here."

"My life is with you." I brush a wet lock of hair away from her cheek to cup it. "I've never been happier than I have been this past week."

"Same." She opens her mouth but hesitates before saying. "But are you sure you want to give this up? It's your home."

"You're my home." I frown then, dropping my hand to my side. "Unless you were planning on keeping this a vacation fling."

"Of course not." She places her palm against my chest.

"I just think we should discuss this more. Not jump to any decisions that can't be undone."

"I have been thinking about this." I rest my forehead against hers. "This place will go back to feeling like a burden the second you leave. I don't mean to put that on you or make you feel guilty. I just want you to know how much you mean to me."

She sighs. "Can we discuss this later? Like maybe over our lunch break. I don't want you to have any regrets."

Regrets that could negatively affect our relationship. I see what she means.

"I can probably put off the developer until then."

"Okay, good." Relief crosses her face. "We can discuss all of this. Together."

Neither of us says much as we dress. Laurel remembers belatedly that she needs to swing by the orchard to pick up something. On her way out, she cups my cheek and leans up to give me a gentle kiss.

"I want to be with you too." Her words lift a weight off my chest. "We'll talk."

When I'm alone, I glance around the house. It's been in my family for generations. But until Laurel started staying over, it didn't feel much like a home. It felt more like a haunted house. Nothing spooky or scary. But a place with memories of the past and what couldn't be.

There's a small crash and I follow the sound to the large family room. Glancing around, it takes me a moment to find the source of the sound.

A picture from the mantle is laying on the floor. My heart skips a beat as I lean to pick it up. I sigh in relief when I see it isn't broken or even cracked. It's a photo of my parents and me. It was taken the year they opened the corn maze for the first time. My parents look so young. Hell, they were probably about the age I am now. In their early to mid-thirties. They look so happy. Like a team.

I guess that's what I remember most about them. They were always together. If there's any small comfort in how they went, it was that they were together. They were always a team. The land might have been my father's, to begin with, but he made Mom a full partner.

That gives me an idea. Setting the frame gently back on top of the mantle, careful to keep it from the edges, I step into the office. I sift through the file cabinet until I find the folder I'm looking for.

Now, I just need to make a quick phone call. Then, I can show Laurel exactly how committed I am to her and us. And that I'm ready to build a life with her, with no regrets.

SEVEN

LAUREL

Staring at my reflection in Olive's bedroom mirror, I nod at myself in approval.

"I definitely look the part," I say, smoothing down the top.

"You look hot." My best friend grins at me from her bed, rubbing her growing belly. "You're going to knock Archer's socks right off of him."

"That's what I'm hoping." I pucker my lips, and in a sultry voice do my best impersonation of Sandy from *Grease*. "'Tell me about it, stud.'"

Olive giggles. "What's bringing all of this on? Are you going to tell him how you feel?"

"Among other things." I turn, facing her then. "But I'll fill you in after. I don't have a minute to lose."

"Go knock him dead."

Olive really is the very best friend. I owe her more than I can say. And not just because she loaned me part of the outfit that is about to play an important part in this scheme I have for Archer. No, she's given me the greatest gift this past week. She's given me the chance to find out who I am and where I'm supposed to be.

Plus, in a way, she introduced me to the man I love. I suppose I'll owe her for that for the rest of my life. And I'm not mad at owing her one for that.

As I set off toward the festival, I think about what I'm about to do. About what I'm going to say to Archer. At first, when he said he wanted to come with me to Boston, I'd been overjoyed. Neither of us had said anything about the future. I'd been afraid to hope this was anything more than a relationship of convenience.

So much for being a confident, independent woman, right?

But when I think about what he's offering to give up for me, it makes me want to cry. He might think it'd be easy to walk away from this love. But I've seen the way he looks when he talks about the land and his home. Right now, it might still feel painful because of all he's lost. I just hope I can show him there are still so many more memories ahead of him. Not all of them will be easy. Not all of them will be perfect. Still, enough of them will be good, it would be a shame to walk away from them.

When I pull up to the grounds my jaw drops. Archer is seated at a table with a gentleman in a suit.

"He better be telling that real estate developer to come back later." I fumble with the buckle. "Otherwise, we're going to have some problems."

I march across the ground. Archer's guest catches sight of me before he does. Based on the appraising once-over he gives me, I'd say he likes my outfit. Well, good. Following his guest's gaze, Archer turns and his eyes go wide.

"Babe." His lips curve into a slow, appreciative grin. "You look good."

"Yes, I know." Of course, I look good. Thanks to a little help from Olive, I've put together an ensemble that could best be described as a sexy lumberjack. "I was hoping it might show you what I'm about to say next."

"Which is?"

"I don't think you should sell the farm." I cover his mouth with my hand before he can interrupt. "I know there are a lot of hard memories. But think about all of the good ones we can make together. I mean, check out this festival. Yeah, I know Olive did a lot of the planning, but we made it even better by working together. And that's just in one week. Think about what we could do in a lifetime together."

Archer's lips spread into a grin against my fingers, sending a flutter through me. "A lifetime together?"

I nod. "We can make a million new memories together. Right here. We can work at it, and leave something behind for the next generations."

"Next generations?" His eyebrows fly up as the light fills his blue eyes. "I like the sound of that."

"Of course you do." But then again, so do I. "We could be really happy here."

He removes my hand from his mouth then and clasps it with both of his. "But what about your job in Boston? Your life there?"

I shake my head. "It's like you said. It doesn't really

feel like home. But you—and me—and all of this. It feels like home."

"So you want to stay?"

"I want to stay." I give a resolute nod. "And I won't let you talk me out of it. Not now that I have an idea for a skincare line and—"

Chuckling, Archer pulls me into his arms as his lips meet mine. Rather than put up a fight so I can finish my thought, I slide my hands over his shoulders and link them behind his neck. This right here is what I'm talking about. It feels right. It feels like home. Sure, there will be things I miss about Boston. But we can always go back for visits. This place is my future. It's captured my heart, right along with the man kissing the breath right out of me.

The sound of someone clearing his throat draws me back to the moment.

Flushing a little, I give him an apologetic look. "Sir, I'm sorry you wasted the time coming here, but the farm isn't for sale."

The man frowns. "I'm not here to buy the farm."

Now it's my turn to stare in confusion. "Then what are you here to do?"

"This is Stanford. The lawyer in town." Archer makes the introductions and waits for us to shake hands. "I was getting his help with some paperwork?"

"What kind of paperwork?"

Archer hands me a folder. I scan over the document quickly and my heart pounds faster with every word. When I've finished reading, I gape at him. "You're making me a co-owner of the farm?"

He nods. "I thought about what you said earlier. About

how we should decide our future together. It was smart. So, I figured you deserved as much of a stake as I have in whatever decision we made."

"You are incredible." I still can't quite believe it. Archer just signed over half of his farm to me. We're equal partners in whatever comes ahead. "I love you. And not just for this."

"Well, I love you too. And not just for this outfit you're wearing." He lowers his voice to whisper in my ear, "I can't wait to see it on the floor of our bedroom later."

I'm laughing when he kisses me again. It's amazing to think about how much life can change in just a few days. A week ago, I thought I was on my way to help a friend and maybe have a fun fall fling. But now, I've found my future. I've found my purpose. I've found the man I want to spend the rest of my life with, and that's better than anything else in the world.

EPILOGUE

ONE YEAR LATER

ARCHER

The loud crash sends me running toward the old barn. We converted it into a 'she shed' for Laurel during the offseason. And ever since, there have been any number of different sights, sounds—and occasionally even smells—coming out of it.

When I called it her witch coven, I ended up spending the night on the couch.

It's the only time in more than six months of marriage that I've been banished to the sofa for a night, so I'll call it a success. Plus, making up the next evening had been more than worth it.

Most of the time, I try to ignore whatever she's up to in there. It keeps things more interesting that way. Plus, after walking in on Laurel, Olive, and Sienna slathering their faces in some green oatmeal looking paste, I figured there are some things a man just doesn't need to know. And whatever she's making in there seems to appeal to our customers.

But in this instance, I feel compelled to check in on her. With only two days to go till the fall festival begins, it's best not to take any chances. Throwing open the barn door, I find Laurel yelling at a straw-filled dummy on the floor.

"Why can't you just look cute, darn it?"

I take a closer look and wince. "Oof. That scarecrow could break mirrors."

It's the wrong thing to say. Her face crumples as tears stream down her face. My stomach hitches and I pull her into my arms.

"It's okay." I rub her back, sparing another glance at the scarecrow. I wince. "We don't need it."

She pulls back suddenly, her eyes wide with surprise. "How can you say that? Of course, we do."

I sigh. These mood swings of hers are going to be the death of me. But they'll be worth it in the end. "We really need another scarecrow?"

"Of course we need one. Not only will it scare off any raccoons who are trying to eat our corn—"

"I'm not really sure there's any science behind that."

"—But the visitors get a kick out of it. And if they get a kick out of it, and our whole fall festival, they'll keep coming back year after year. And if they come back year after year—"

"Let me guess, they'll bring their friends. Which will mean more business."

"Exactly. And we want more business. Not because we're greedy. But because we're building a legacy for this little guy or gal." She runs her hand over her belly, sending a wave of warmth through me.

Grinning, I reach over to cover her hand. "I still can't quite believe it."

Her expression softens. "I can't either."

She wants everything to be perfect so we can build a legacy for the family we're making together. One that we've already started. Can I really argue with her for wanting to do that?

"Where do you want to hang the scarecrow."

She claps her hands together, her expression turning from a frown to a smile in a flash. "I know just the spot. It's a little bit of a hike, but it shouldn't take us too long."

"Just let me grab my toolbox." I hitch the scarecrow under one arm and sling the other over her shoulders. "Then you show me the way."

I have a feeling this is how it'll be for the next fifty or so autumns. She'll give me my marching orders. I'll grumble a little. But then I'll do exactly what she suggests because she's usually right. Besides, we're in this together. We're a team. We're a family.

We have a million memories to make in the years ahead of us. I'm looking forward to living each and every one of them.

Thank you for reading!

Want to read more?

Click here to receive a FREE spicy romance short read.

Want updates on new and upcoming releases?

Follow me on BookBub and subscribe to my newsletter.

Want to connect?

Find me on Facebook, Instagram, TikTok, YouTube, and Kate Tilney's Mountain Man (Etc.) Fan Club.

Want to be an ultimate fan?

Get audiobooks and bargain bundles on my site or shop tie-in merch on Bonfire. You can also join In Bed with Kate Tilney and Lana Dash on Ream for exclusive stories and bonus content you won't find anywhere else.

Turn the page for more reads from yours truly...

ALSO BY KATE TILNEY

Kings of the Mountain

Instalove Weekend

Ridiculously Royal

Sunset Canyon Fire & Rescue: The Veterans

Sunset Canyon Fire & Rescue: The Rookies

Camp Mountain Man

Shipwrecked Beach Babes

Jade Mountain Search & Rescue

Lancaster Ranch Cowboys

Love at the Fall Festival

The Firefighters Calendar

Mountain Man Animal Rescue Volume 1

Mountain Man Animal Rescue Volume 2

Prince Family Mountain Men

Curvy Girl and the Billionaire

Holidays with a Mountain Man

Mountain Man Fan Club

The Curvy Girls' Bachelor Auction Volume 1

Curvy Girls' Bucket List

A Short, Sweet, and Steamy Christmas

Blame It on the Vodka

Firth Mountain Smokejumpers

Fudge It All

Holly and the Ghost of Christmas Present

A Baby for the Mountain Man

Milton Keynes UK
Ingram Content Group UK Ltd.
UKHW010647021023
429777UK00004B/304